SOUL HUNTER
THE LAST IMMORTAL

alex MARLOWE

LB

LITTLE, BROWN BOOKS FOR YOUNG READERS
www.lbkids.co.uk

LITTLE, BROWN BOOKS FOR YOUNG READERS

First published in Great Britain in 2016 by Hodder and Stoughton

1 3 5 7 9 10 8 6 4 2

A CIP catalogue record for this book
is available from the British Library.

ISBN 978-0-349-13182-5

Typeset in Caslon by M Rules
Printed and bound in Great Britain by
Clays Ltd, St Ives plc

The paper and board used in this book are made from
wood from responsible sources.

MIX
Paper from
responsible sources
FSC® C104740

Little, Brown Books for Young Readers
An imprint of
Hachette Children's Group
Part of Hodder and Stoughton
Carmelite House
50 Victoria Embankment
London EC4Y 0DZ

An Hachette UK Company
www.hachette.co.uk

www.lbkids.co.uk

For the Snowdon boys

With special thanks to Michael Ford

CHAPTER 1

Louisiana, 1842

Trees clawing at a blood-red sky. Swampland threading out among the mangroves like silver ribbons. An unnatural silence. The predawn air was cool, but it would be sticky soon.

Aurora Cage tossed her coin, spoke the names of the dead in her mind.

Persephone. Poor sweet Persephone.

Left and right, the other werewolves moved into position among the trees. She tossed the coin again.

Brother Hector. A good man. Too good to die like that.

An egret unfolded itself from a half-submerged log, a fish twisting in its long beak. Its wingbeats reached her like whispers.

Aurora flipped the coin again, heart hardening.

Europa. Just a girl. Twelve summers old.

She sniffed the air, and the flooded land gave off its scents. Wolf, obviously – mixed with sour human sweat. A pine trunk, split open and giving off the tang of bitter sap. Raccoon droppings. The promise of rain.

And there, very faint, but setting her pulse racing, a creature that didn't belong – rich blood, muscle, flesh.

Draka – the Soul Hunter. Not far away now.

Aurora sent the coin spinning a fourth time – for little Lysidas, her eight-year-old nephew.

A meaty hand whipped out and snatched the coin from the air.

"Would you quit that?"

Aurora didn't turn. She knew the voice. It was Thane. Her nostrils filled with the musty stink of the coney pelts that lined his jacket. She held out her hand towards him, the hairs across her neck bristling. "I'd give that back if I were you."

"Or what?" he replied. He was trying to sound cocky, but her nose picked up the smell of his fear.

She cocked her head towards him – a wiry dark-haired man, teeth discoloured from the tobacco he constantly chewed. She growled. "Or you won't be in a position to do anything."

After a pause, he discharged a gobbet of brown spit on to the ground and dropped the coin into her palm.

Aurora hadn't known Thane more than a couple of

weeks. He'd not been turned long, bitten while out hunting with his buddies, apparently. *He* had become the hunted when he ran into the pack under a full moon. He was still too cocky for his own good, the new wolf spirit pumping through his veins.

But he had no idea what the coin meant to her.

"You'll have plenty of compensation when all this is over," said Aurora.

"Damn right," said Thane. He rubbed his hands together greedily. Aurora didn't blame him for that either. Fact was, the whole pack, apart from her, was here for the gold. The mayor of the city had turned to them to rid the swamps of Draka, and he was willing to pay handsomely.

"You think he even came this way?" said Thane, changing the subject. "We ain't seen a track for two whole days."

Aurora narrowed her eyes. The sky was turning pink. Sun would be up soon. The first of the tree frogs began their chorus. "I can smell him," she said.

They'd been trailing their prey for almost a week, from the outskirts of New Orleans and the massacre at the church. Time was, Draka would have stuck to the fishing communities, striking only at isolated river dwellings, or the native tribes that still rode across the plains. But he was getting more brave, preferring the rich pickings of the city slums. Or, Aurora thought with a sudden stab of grief, the farms and plantation houses that spread out from the delta.

Houses like the one where her brother's family had lived.

She tried to put a wall up in her mind, but the images were too powerful. She closed her eyes, and tried to breathe easy as they assailed her.

The swing hanging from the ironwood in the front yard, moving gently in the breeze. Everything too quiet. No music from the old piano. No sawing from the woodshed. No children laughing.

The splintered front door.

She'd called their names, quiet at first as she'd walked through the wreck of the front room with the furniture all tipped around. One of her brother's fine-turned chairs was smashed to bits. Her calls turned to shouts of panic as she swept up the stairs.

And then she'd found them, in the children's bedroom.

Her brother had put up a fight. She found his axe, the blade crusted brown with blood at his feet, the shaft broken in two. He hadn't stood a chance against Draka.

Their bodies were all there – they'd died together, her brother Hector clutching little Europa in his arms. The girl's eyes were still open, face etched with the terror of her last moments.

Aurora had stooped beside them, speechless and sick, to close Europa's eyes. Only then had she seen her niece was still clutching something in her palm. She'd prised open

4

the cold stiff fingers and found the silver dime inside. The so-called lucky coin she'd given Europa a few days before, on her birthday.

So much for good fortune. So much for protecting her kin.

"Hey, Cage, you all right?" said Thane.

Aurora came back to the present. Her hand hurt from gripping the coin so tightly it dug into the flesh of her palm.

"I will be," she said, "when I've finished with Draka."

A twig snapped behind them, and they both turned as Red Fur came forwards in a crouch.

"Getting sloppy," said Aurora.

The Alpha glowered at her, then grinned. He swigged from a flask, water droplets dripping off his thick moustache. Apart from Carlos, he was the oldest of the pack, turned during the War of Independence sixty years before and cursed never to age a day over forty. He still wore the rags of his uniform – a filthy mustard waistcoat with a tattered and patched blue coat. His sabre hung at his side.

"Never mind me," said Red Fur. "Where's the damned witch?"

Aurora scanned the swamp. She could see – and smell – the other werewolves. But Marie Le Roux was nowhere to be seen.

"She'll be here," said Aurora. "She promised."

"A witch's promise ain't worth squat," said Thane. "Why'd we trust her, anyhow?"

"She promised," said Aurora again.

"I say we go in now," said Thane. "We don't need some old lady."

Red Fur sighed patiently. Aurora wondered if it was going to be up to her to put Thane in his place at some point. He had no respect for the hierarchy of the pack.

"I'm just saying," continued Thane.

"Maybe you should try bein' quiet," said a woman's voice.

Now they all jumped. Marie Le Roux, dressed in a brown shawl, crouched in the fork of a nearby tree. Aurora hadn't even scented her.

"How long you been there?" said Thane, stuffing more tobacco into his cheek.

"Long enough to hear you callin' me an ol' lady," said Marie. She jumped down, landing surprisingly lightly for a woman of seventy-odd years. Her wrinkled skin stretched into a smile at Aurora. "You think you ready to take on Draka?"

"I'll tear him to pieces," said Thane, butting in. He drew a hunting knife from inside his boot, and the blade glistened wickedly.

Marie Le Roux chuckled. "You ain't got an inkling."

"You reckon you do?" Thane began. "I'll—"

"Just listen to her," said Red Fur.

The witch strode towards them. "You think that lil' knife gonna cause hurt to Draka? You can't cut him, boy. He don't

6

bleed like a man. You can't shoot him with no gun. You can't burn him with no fire. Sure, you might keep him down for a lil' while, but he ain't from this world. He can heal hisself, and he always come back stronger."

"So you say," muttered Thane.

"I seen it," said Marie. "I know what he can do."

"And that's why you're here," said Red Fur. "I trust you're prepared."

Marie clenched her toothless jaws. "Just take care of your own, moon-chile."

Red Fur put his hands around his mouth and mimicked perfectly the shrill call of a whooping crane. Across the swamps, the wolf pack began to move towards the spit of wooded land ahead.

When Aurora looked back at Marie, the witch had gone.

Aurora moved too, stepping out into a narrow channel of water, testing the depth with each step. The others moved silently through the ripples. The level only came as high as Aurora's waist before the ground started to rise again. She was pleased that Thane had decided to shut his mouth for a while.

They reached dry land on the other side. The skin tingled on the back of Aurora's neck. The air seemed different here. Colder, despite the sun now filtering through the branches of the trees. Bare branches, like the trees were rotting from the ground up. The stench of decay.

Aurora unslung the Springfield from her back, and

checked the chamber again. She'd heard Marie well enough, but it still made her feel better to have a pouch of musket balls and powder. She knew the damage she could do with a clean shot. And it was up to them to keep Draka busy while Marie worked her magic.

Plans were one thing, carrying them out was another.

She saw a tree ahead, its trunk daubed with blood and entrails. A warning, maybe. There were others too, gouged with claw marks half an inch deep. Red Fur, to her right, gave hand signals to fan out.

Gold and the promise of more had brought the pack this far, but Aurora wondered how Thane and the other wolves would react when they saw their enemy at last.

So far they were keeping formation.

Aurora knew *she* would never back down. Not until Hector and his family were avenged.

The mangrove trees were dead here, crowded together but blackened and drooping. She saw animal skulls – dogs and cats – hanging by pieces of frayed twine. They spun slowly, eye sockets revolving. There were skins too, buzzing with flies. The smells became more pungent and powerful.

Then a voice spoke, deep and gravelly, with no accent Aurora had ever heard before. "So you come to me at last, half-bloods."

All the werewolves stopped in their tracks, looking this way and that. Thane's hand trembled as he cocked his gun.

"Show yourself!" said Red Fur. He stepped into the clearing ahead, and drew his sabre.

Aurora scanned the undergrowth.

"Very well," said the voice.

A sudden movement, dead ahead. Adam, a stable boy before he was turned, looked up in shock, as something dropped from the branches above him. His cry was cut short as Draka's foot crushed his skull into the ground. Everyone jumped back, and Aurora felt bile rise in her throat.

She swallowed it back as she stared at the Soul Hunter. Draka wasn't quite twice the height of a man, but he must have been ten feet tall. His skin, where Aurora could see it, was blood red. Much of it – his forearms, legs and chest – was covered by a flexing second skin, black-green, with a sort of shimmer. He wore a helmet of bone – the skull of a bull, perhaps, with horns curving upwards. Yellow eyes, with slitted black pupils, stared from behind the skull's sockets and made Aurora shudder with the depth of their animal cunning. More skulls, smaller ones, hung from his neck on a cord.

Across his shoulder was a bow, which looked as if it was made from two huge rib bones joined in the centre.

The creature's chest heaved, and he reached behind his back with a clawed hand and took out an arrow from a quiver, three feet long. Aurora shivered, despite herself, when she saw the tip glinting with silver – werewolves' weakness.

He was expecting us.

Aurora herself was immune to the metal, courtesy of a werewolf hunter's silver musket bullet that had left a scar on her cheek, and a trace of silver in her blood. But it wouldn't help the others.

Under Draka's foot, Adam moved weakly, one hand twitching. Somehow he was still alive. Draka flipped the arrow over his hand, then thumped the point into the fallen werewolf's chest. Adam spasmed and Draka opened his mouth, breathing in a long slow breath, chest rising. Adam's jerking body began to glow. A pale light leaked from his wound like a swirl of smoke. It shimmered in the air, reminding Aurora of a patch of rippling moonlight in a pool. *Adam's spirit.* Draka opened his mouth wide, his teeth jagged points. With a contented sigh, he sucked the floating spirit towards him. It writhed in the air, like it was trying to resist. But the pull was too strong. With a final intake of breath, the spirit disappeared down Draka's throat. Adam lay still at last, the light gone from his body.

So that's how he got his name, thought Aurora, sickened. She imagined Hector and his family having their spirits sucked from them and consumed by this monster. She curled her fists, her claw-like nails cutting into her palms, drawing blood. Pure rage swept through her.

"Who is next?" said the Soul Hunter.

CHAPTER 2

"Attack!" bellowed Red Fur.

Aurora leapt in. The other werewolves charged from every side.

Draka moved more quickly than Aurora would have thought possible. He crouched and scooped Adam's limp body with one hand, hurling it at the oncoming wolves. It slammed into Cole and Tanner, sending them sprawling. Then Draka drew another arrow, stringing it to his bow. He turned and fired at Aurora.

She ducked, dropping into a slide, and the arrow flew past. She saw it strike Oakum in the throat, lifting him off his feet and pinning him to the trunk of a tree. His eyes were wide with shock and blood poured over his fingers as he reached for the wound. Then his arms fell to his sides, and he slumped forwards, dead. His body spasmed and glowed as his flickering spirit was drawn out by the Soul Hunter.

Aurora watched, mesmerised, as the sparkling cloud snaked through the air towards Draka and, with a final inhale, was sucked into the red demon's mouth.

Aurora threw herself, full force, at the Soul Hunter. It was like smashing into a wall. He staggered back a fraction, but stayed on his feet. Aurora dodged the first swipe of his claws, but the second caught her leg, spinning her upside down. She found herself thrown twenty feet across the clearing, and only when she landed with a splash in shallow water did she feel the pain. Her thigh was gouged and pumping out blood. An artery. Hell, it hurt!

Cole, recovered but with a bleeding scalp, reached her side. He was a woodsman, as tough as they came.

"Aurora!" he said.

"I'm OK," she replied. "Leave me!"

She ripped the sleeve off her jacket with her teeth and began to fasten the scrap of cloth around the top of her injured leg.

Cole nodded and leapt up to join the others in the attack.

Aurora cried out in pain as she yanked the tourniquet tight. An arrow sliced the air every few seconds, and there were already two other werewolves on the ground. Doug was down. Anya too. Zander had an arrow in his shoulder and yanked it out, only for another to go right through his belly. He collapsed on to his knees and died, crouched over, right in front of Aurora. She blinked, dazzled, as his bright glimmering soul wound up into the night air. With one icy heave of breath, it was devoured by Draka, triumph glinting in his glassy eyes.

She was sure their enemy had grown a foot or two. Now she looked closer, she realised the armour he wore was alligator skin. They didn't stand a chance with blades against something that tough.

She saw her gun lying on the ground, and reached for it with a blood-streaked hand.

She cocked the hammer and brought the barrel round. Red Fur was in the way, swinging his sabre. Cole too. Draka kicked Cole aside and turned, reaching out with an arm to block Red Fur's blade. It connected, biting deep into the creature's elbow, in the gap between two plates of alligator armour. The limb split open and the forearm fell to the ground with a heavy thud, still holding the bone bow.

Draka shrieked with pain and hope surged through Aurora's heart.

But as Red Fur swung again, this time at Draka's head, Draka moved in. The blade sparked off the bull's skull helmet, and flew out of his hand. Aurora saw the Soul Hunter's single hand coming up, clutching an arrow.

"Look out!"

Red Fur glanced down just as the arrow's point drove through his middle. It burst from the back of his soldier's jacket, covered in gore.

"No!" screamed Aurora.

Red Fur fell back into the mud, blood welling at his mouth. Draka stood triumphant over his body, chest swelling as he sucked in a long rasping breath. The werewolf leader shook on the ground, his limbs thumping against the damp earth, his body glowing. A pale reddish light formed above the Alpha, writhing as it was drawn towards the Soul Hunter. And then it vanished into Draka's gaping mouth. Red Fur lay completely still.

Aurora fired the musket with a muzzle flash and a cloud of smoke, right at Draka's head. She heard the round hit home and saw fragments of bone explode. Draka twisted and fell, breaking his fall with his remaining hand. He rose to his feet and shook his head groggily.

The lower portion of the bull's jaw was gone, fractured by the musket ball. Beneath it Aurora saw the Hunter's red face, human but not so. Draka had no lips, and his nose was just two gaping nostrils. Sinews and muscle without skin, stretched over the shards of teeth.

Draka's eyes passed over her, and he held the bleeding stump of his arm towards where his severed hand lay on the ground. Aurora swallowed to stop herself retching as the fingers flexed. How was that even possible? Then the forearm moved, sliding across the ground towards Draka. He crouched, picked it up and held the two ragged wounds against each other.

Aurora shook her head as the arm began to knit together.

Marie Le Roux was right. He's indestructible.

He turned to face her, and the goat-eyes blazed with anger. "I will feast on your soul, wolf-woman," he said.

He took a step towards Aurora. Her fingers fumbled with the powder for a second shot. She could normally get off three rounds a minute, maybe four. She snapped the barrel closed and reached for a ball, but dropped it. Draka leapt at her, claws reaching for her face. Aurora rolled away and heard the tree where she'd been resting take the impact. Draka growled in frustration.

She scrambled up to her feet, and almost passed out with the pain from her leg. Taking the gun by the barrel, she swung it like a club at Draka's head. He caught the stock easily and yanked it from her, then tossed the gun aside.

Aurora was hobbling backwards, and with each step her leg threatened to give way. She looked round for a weapon. Red Fur's sabre lay on the ground, ten feet away. Too far.

Draka seemed to be enjoying the moment, stalking his prey, lipless mouth twisted into a smile. He drew a long knife from his belt, and his other hand shot up and gripped her around the throat. He lifted her until her feet left the ground. "Your fear will make you taste sweeter," he said.

Aurora began to choke as the claws squeezed her neck, but her terror gave way to anger. Was this terrible face what her innocent nephew and niece had seen, before they died? Her brother and his wife too, at the mercy of this *thing*? She reached into her pocket and closed her fist around the coin. She wouldn't give him the satisfaction of being afraid.

The Soul Hunter raised his long knife above Aurora's throat.

"Just get this over with," she wheezed.

Draka jerked as Cole appeared on his back, burying his teeth into the red neck, shaking his head back and forth and ripping at the shoulder. The knife fell to the ground as Draka squirmed. His grip on Aurora's neck loosened and she dropped in a heap. The pain that shot up her leg made her scream. Draka was spinning, trying to throw Cole off, reaching up and over with his clawed hands, but the werewolf didn't let go. He was tearing away chunks of skin and flesh, like a mad dog.

Aurora crawled across the ground on her hands and knees towards Red Fur's sword. It might be her only chance.

The Soul Hunter stepped backwards into a tree, crushing Cole against it. He didn't let go.

Aurora's fist closed around the sabre's hilt. She stabbed its point into the mud and pushed herself upright.

Draka slammed Cole again. This time his head hit the trunk. With a groan, he let go and slumped to the ground. The Soul Hunter turned on him, drawing an arrow with his hand.

Throwing all her weight behind the blow, Aurora struck. The sabre sliced three-quarters through Draka's standing leg and, as she pulled it out in a shower of blood, the leg folded underneath him. Draka landed on both hands. Aurora drew back the blade again, eyes fixed on the exposed and torn flesh of his neck.

Draka's yellow eyes glanced up. "No . . ." he managed to growl.

And with a roar of triumph, Aurora brought the sabre down.

The blade cleaved clean through the muscle and bone with a *thunk*. Draka's head rolled free, and came to rest face down a few feet away. There was a pause, before the giant body toppled sideways and lay curled in a ball.

Aurora let the sword hang for a moment, breathing heavily.

Cole, still up against the tree, grinned through a mouth coated in Draka's blood. "Not bad, Cage," he said. "I guess I owe you."

"I'd say we're even," said Aurora. She offered a hand, and he took it. She winced as she helped him to his feet. The leg still hurt like hell, but it would heal, she knew – that was part of what it meant to be immortal.

Thane came out of the trees, clutching his arm and limping. "We did it," he said, a slight tremble in his voice.

Aurora looked at him. Apart from some torn clothing, and a mud-streak across his cheek, she couldn't see much wrong with him.

"And where were *you*?" asked Cole.

Anger flashed across Thane's face. "I was in the first attack," he said. "Got in a coupl'a shots, but he knocked me clean out. Too bad about Red Fur, huh?"

Aurora followed his gaze across the clearing, surveying the carnage. Red Fur, Adam, Oakum, Anya, Doug, Zander. All dead. Tanner was moving weakly, but his back was broken by the looks of it. More than half the pack was gone. "Looks like Cage was 'bout right," muttered Thane. "Ol' Red Fur was gettin' sloppy."

Aurora's fingers clenched around the sword hilt. "Careful what you say, coward."

Thane suddenly seemed to forget about his injured arm, and drew his hunting knife, squaring up. "What d'you call me?"

"Wait!" said Cole, putting a hand in front of Aurora. She batted it aside.

"Red Fur had more guts in his little finger than you've got in your whole body," she snarled. She tossed the sword aside. She could take a pup like Thane with just her bare hands.

"No, wait! Look!" said Cole, pointing at the ground. "It's moving!"

Aurora forgot about Thane in an instant. Cole was right. Draka's head, still covered with the bone helmet, was wobbling from side to side. With jerking movements, it began to drag itself towards the headless red corpse.

"What the—" muttered Thane.

Aurora lifted a foot and placed it on top of the head. She could feel it moving beneath the sole of her boot, like some living thing trying to escape.

"Allow me," said a woman's voice. Marie Le Roux appeared across the clearing. "Stand back."

"'Bout time you showed up," said Thane, backing away.

Aurora stepped off the head.

Marie was waving one open hand in front of her, as if manipulating some invisible object. Her other hand was closed above her, reaching for the sky. Her lips moved too, chanting under her breath in one long stream of sound, seemingly unbroken by the need to breathe. Her eyes fixed on the body of the Soul Hunter.

Clouds swept across the sky, black and angry, and impossibly fast. Lightning flashed in their depths. The witch reached up high, then brought her hand down in a jerking motion. Lightning forked, bright enough that Aurora had to throw up her hands, and even then the flash blinded her behind her clenched eyes. The crash was so loud she expected the earth to open up under her feet, and she felt the heat across her skin. The static made her hair shoot up across her body.

When she opened her eyes again, the clearing was just the same, but for the branches swaying. A white smoke rose from Draka's body like mist. Aurora just about made out the dim shape of twisting limbs within the swirling cloud as it lifted into the air.

Aurora realised what it was. *The soul of Draka.*

Marie Le Roux was shaking from head to foot, her eyes rolled back in her head. The spirit of the Soul Hunter seemed to want to cling to its body, but Marie was straining with her closed fist, as if dragging the spirit towards her. Then, like a spider's web pulled apart, the mist relinquished its grip on the body and flowed towards her all at once, sucked into her clenched fist.

Marie's eyes returned to normal, and she sagged under her shawl. "It is done," she said. "Draka's soul and body are severed. He will not live again."

Thane brushed his clothes down. "So you say, ol' woman." He walked over cautiously to Draka's head, then raised his boot to kick it. He jumped back. "It moved!"

The head was still twitching, being pulled towards the Soul Hunter's corpse.

"It's still got its power," said Marie. "Nothing can destroy it."

Thane spat on the ground. "I say we burn the body, just to make damn sure."

"You ain't learnt nothin'," said Marie. "I told you – it will always regenerate, even from ash. The body has been a vessel for Soul Hunters since ancient times. The Blood Armour, it's called. Many other Soul Hunters inhabited it before Draka, and many have tried to destroy it. It can't be done. Let me take care of it."

"What will you do?" asked Aurora.

Marie touched the side of her nose. "Don't you worry about that, chile," she said. "Go now, tend to your injured. It's done."

It took them until the sun was noon-high to bury the bodies. By that time, Aurora's leg had healed completely, but it still ached dully as she shovelled the last piles of earth on to Red Fur's mound. They burned Draka's skulls and hides, while Marie continued her secret rituals with the Blood Armour, spreading rune stones around it in a circle, waving a smoking branch, and muttering her strange chants.

Aurora threw on the final spadeful, then stared at Red Fur's grave. *It's how he'd have wanted to die – with the pack*, she thought.

Cole came past with Tanner. "How's the back?" she said.

"Been better," said Tanner, stretching. He looked at the line of graves. "Where to now, boss?" he said.

His words took a moment to sink in. Was he talking to her?

"What d'you mean?" she replied.

"We need a new Alpha," said Tanner.

"Hold up, there," said Thane. "What d'you mean? We can't have no woman leadin' us."

"Shut your mouth, Thane," said Tanner.

"I'm just sayin'—"

"Well, don't," said Cole.

"We don't need to talk about this now," said Aurora. She was tired. "The other packs need to be told what's happened. Let's hold a council on the next full moon."

Cole and Tanner nodded and glared at Thane.

"Sure," he said grumpily. "Sure thing."

Only Aurora had already decided. By the next full moon she'd be gone.

This place held nothing for her now. Her family was avenged, but they'd never be coming back. Sure, the mayor of New Orleans had paid off the pack, but soon it would be business as normal, and werewolves would be fair game once more. She needed a fresh start – somewhere completely different. She even had somewhere in mind. If she could face the seasickness, it might be just what she needed.

"Let's go home," she said.

They set off, back towards the swamps, as the sun blazed down.

Aurora let herself fall behind, and that was when Marie Le Roux caught up.

"You forgot this," the witch said, and held out the silver dime. Aurora automatically reached for her pocket, then realised she must have dropped it in the fight with Draka. But when the witch placed it in her open palm, Aurora knew at once there was something different about the coin. It felt heavier, somehow.

"You need to look after this," said Marie. "Keep it close."

Aurora frowned. "Why?"

A rustle in the trees ahead made her look up. But it was only Thane, peering suspiciously back at them.

"Because if you don't," said the witch, folding Aurora's huge hand in her wrinkled fingers, "a lot of folks are gonna die."

CHAPTER 3

London, present day

The ocular lens chip Harker had implanted into Luke's right eye performed several functions. With just a thought, it could slow things down, like lagging the frame-rate of reality. Vampires did it naturally, of course – that accounted for their quick reactions. But Luke's chip could zoom too, up to sixty times.

He used both tools now as he watched the coin leave Aurora's hand in slow motion, spinning upwards. It caught the gold reflection of a street light, and he saw each side in turn. A seated woman on one side, a wreath on the other, dated 1833. Aurora's famous silver dime, which she carried everywhere with her.

"Hey, focus, will you?" said Evelyn, flicking her long black hair from her face. "We don't have long."

Luke returned to his scrapbook and the half-finished drawing of the corpse in front of him. The dead woman was sprawled across the ground, limbs at unnatural angles, rivulets of blood from her head already coalescing stickily among the cobblestones. She wore a smart white coat, ankle-length, and high-heeled shoes.

"You want a professional opinion?" said Aurora, still tossing the coin and casting nervous glances up and down the alley. "She's dead."

Luke crouched closer for a better view of the woman's head, which was oddly misshapen. "A crushed skull will do that to a person," he said. He tried to capture the contours accurately with his pencil. "Gross, huh?"

Evelyn looked at him with raised eyebrows. "Gross? Not a very *you* word," she said. "Shouldn't a Victorian say something like 'abominable'?"

"Just trying to fit in," said Luke. Actually, he'd been about to say "ghastly", but his contemporary vocabulary upload had kicked in.

From above them came a grinding sound and a shower of stony fragments rained down. Luke glanced up and saw Raziel perched on the office building's parapet four storeys high, his wings folded. His head turned to them and Luke heard his rumbling voice through the earpiece he wore. "I've seen a police car," he said. "Siren's quiet. Three minutes away at most."

"Great!" said Aurora, throwing out her arms.

Luke sketched faster.

"Don't want to interrupt the art class or anything," said Evelyn, "but maybe we should take some samples too?" She frowned. "I wonder where Dad's got to."

"He's close," said Aurora, pocketing the coin. "I can smell him."

Evelyn, on her knees, snipped some of the victim's hair, and took a pipette to the blood pool. Luke saw her lick her lips – only natural for a vampire, he guessed.

A moment later, they heard the clicking of Harker's cane and he hobbled around the corner of the alley. "Sorry," he said. "Just talking to our friend, Dustin."

Luke smiled. Harker seemed to have contacts everywhere in the city, and Luke wasn't surprised that the street-dweller they'd seen earlier was another in the pay of the Immortals.

"And?" said Evelyn.

"He can't tell us much more," said Harker, coming closer and peering at the body. "He heard howling, and growling. Thought it was a dog fight at first, but then he came across the body. Saw three figures running away. Called us."

Now Harker was in the light, Luke could see him better. It was hard to believe that just a couple of months ago, Jonathan Harker had been a strong man and fearsome vampire, capable of physical feats that had made Luke gasp. The scrapbook in his hands contained detailed records of

Harker's abilities. Leaping twenty metres from a building without making a sound, lifting up to three times his own body-weight, nails that could tear through wood with ease . . .

He was thinner than ever now, with black shadows under his eyes. He was out of his wheelchair, at least, but it looked like his legs would snap if he moved too quickly. His thick dark hair had turned almost completely white in the months since his ordeal, and Luke was embarrassed to see Harker's blotchy scalp beneath, as the Immortals' leader bent down to study the corpse. Evelyn, he realised, had caught him looking, and he turned quickly away, back to the body.

It must be even harder for her. Seeing her dad like this.

"It was probably just muggers," said Aurora.

"Perhaps," said Harker. "Turn the body over."

Aurora stooped down, her long duster coat pooling on the ground, and gently eased the woman's body over. Luke gasped. He hadn't been expecting *that*.

She was covered in blood, from scratches across her face and neck, and deeper gouges in her chest. "Definitely *homo lupus*," said Luke. "Look at the spacing between the cuts."

Aurora's brow furrowed, and he knew she was troubled. "It makes no sense. It's not even a full moon."

"She fought back," said Evelyn, pointing to the woman's pale fingernails, caked with blood.

Luke zoomed in with his ocular lens. "Wait a minute . . ."

He crouched beside Evelyn, and touched the corpse's cold hands. Then he grabbed the finger.

"What are you doing?" said Evelyn.

She winced as Luke flipped off the nail. "Fake," he said. Beneath the acrylic nail was a real one. It was a shade too dark to be human, and ended in a taper. Luke let the hand drop, then reached for the dead woman's head. He pushed back her upper lip slightly with the butt of his pencil. The canines were a fraction too long as well. "She's a werewolf too," he said.

"Weird," said Aurora. "I didn't smell it – must be her perfume." She dropped suddenly over the body, on all fours like a cat. She brought her nose close, and sniffed deeply. "You're right, Luke." She paused, then reached for a necklace slightly visible under the woman's collar, and tugged it out. On it was a pendant. Luke began to sketch at once – it was a simple disc of metal, marked with a line down the middle.

"*Canes umbrarum*," muttered Aurora.

"Sorry?" said Evelyn. "My Latin's rusty."

"Shadow dogs," said Luke.

The sound of running feet made them all look up. A police officer skidded around the corner, and Luke's heart stopped, eyes quickly scanning for a means of escape. Then the officer whipped off his hat and Luke saw it was only Dodger with his ever-grubby young face and wispy beard.

"We gotta get out of here," he said. "Old Bill are coming."

Harker glanced up. "Raziel, back to the base."

The gargoyle spread his wings and took off.

"Where'd you get the outfit?" said Luke, stuffing his scrapbook into his satchel and shouldering it. He'd added an extra strap so he could carry it like a rucksack.

Dodger tapped his nose. "A magician doesn't reveal his secrets," he said. "I needed something that would let me have a nose around."

"And?" said Harker, as he began to limp with the rest of them towards the other end of the alley.

"Few scraped cars, broken windows. If I had to guess, I'd reckon they chased her through the streets and caught her 'ere."

"Any CCTV cameras?" asked Harker.

"Nope," said Dodger. "We're clear, guv." He pulled off the police uniform and dropped it in a bin along with the hat. Beneath he was wearing his normal crumpled black trousers and buttoned waistcoat.

Luke realised Aurora wasn't with them. He looked back and saw her still standing in the alley, staring at the body. He whistled, and she took a moment to follow.

"I'll speak to my people at the Met," said Harker. "See if I can get any more information once the full autopsy is complete. We'll analyse our samples too, just to be sure."

They'd reached the main road, where he raised a hand

to hail a black cab. As one pulled over, the driver wound down the window. The jingle of a radio station drifted out. "Where to?" the driver asked.

"Southwark Cathedral," said Harker.

They climbed in, and Luke saw the driver giving them a strange glance. They were a funny-looking bunch, to say the least. Aurora clambered inside last, and the cab's suspension dipped as she settled down next to Luke.

"Fancy-dress party, is it?" said the driver, grinning at her long duster coat and rancher's hat.

Aurora glared back at him in the rear-view mirror, her scar twisting across her cheek. The driver's smile fell from his face.

After they'd been travelling a few minutes, Evelyn spoke up. "Who are the *canes umbrarum*?"

"A pack of—" Luke began.

Harker held up a frail hand. "Wait a moment." He leaned forwards and asked the driver, "Would you mind turning it up? It's my favourite song." The driver grunted and adjusted the volume. His voice now disguised under the blare of music, Harker muttered, "Go on."

"They're a pack of werewolves," said Luke. "I remember Dad telling me about them. Originally based in Paris in the 1700s. But they moved to London in the early nineteenth century."

Aurora nodded. "They've been in London since after

the Napoleonic Wars," she said. "They went straight. Lived normal lives, as much as they could."

"Yeah, that woman looked like a lawyer, or a banker, something like that," said Luke.

"The question is, why was she killed?" asked Harker.

As the taxi went over a speed hump, Evelyn's father grimaced in pain.

"You all right, Dad?"

"Yes," he said, his eyes closed in a long blink.

"I told you that you shouldn't have come," Evelyn said. "You need more rest."

"I'll be fine," said Harker, but Luke could see his knuckles were still white as they gripped the tip of his cane. He was struggling, and Luke wished for the umpteenth time he could do something to help.

"She was an innocent," growled Aurora. "She didn't deserve to die like that. There will be revenge."

"A werewolf war?" said Dodger. "Right, I'm stayin' indoors."

Luke felt a shiver of fear, laced with excitement. Part of him shared Dodger's wish to lie low, but another ... well, if there were going to be werewolves fighting in the streets of London, he wanted to *see* it. Besides, he'd signed the pledge of the Immortals, his last promise to his father. To fight evil wherever it arose.

In the months since defeating the undead pharaoh

Sanakhte, the Immortals had completed a number of missions, some more dangerous than others. Tracking down a group of sewer trolls with a taste for Londoners was pretty cool. The creatures had been appearing along the banks of the Thames, snatching victims from the riverside. Luke had worked out the likely culprits using gait analysis, as well as his own report written in the 1850s when his father was kidnapped by one of the hulking creatures. This time, the Immortals had tracked the offenders to a lair in West London, where a battle had ensued. The evil hypnotist de Guerlain had been a challenge, too – he'd almost convinced Luke to drown himself. But so far there'd been nothing as big as a werewolf war.

The taxi dropped them off on Southwark Bridge, and the Gothic spires of the cathedral were silhouetted against the sky. Raziel, completely motionless, crouched against a hanging buttress already. In the day it was so busy here you could barely walk the pavements without bumping into people, but now, at three in the morning, a sort of peace reigned. Granted, there were a few shift-workers on night buses, delivery vans and drunks. The odd fox stalking brazenly through the streets. But it was as quiet as the city of London got.

Evelyn hung back as the others made their way towards the graveyard.

"You OK?" asked Luke.

Evelyn shook her head, and took a deep breath. Luke

thought she might even be about to cry, but she didn't. "I'm worried about Dad," she said. "He's not getting better."

Luke didn't know what to say. He'd been frantically searching through his father's papers for information about Blood Deprivation Syndrome and its effects. The problem was that many of Victor Frankenstein's books had been lost in a fire in the 1960s, and there was nothing left about a possible cure for the illness. Luke knew the basics from Evelyn, who had heard of a case once. Apparently, BDS was a vampire disease brought on when the subject was unable to feed for a sustained period of time. A vampire's need for blood was a bit like a human's need for water, but it was psychological as well as physical. Just as prolonged dehydration could damage a person's liver and kidneys, being deprived of blood could wreak havoc on a vampire's physiology. And, after a while, the body began to attack itself in its need for sustenance.

The ordeal that Sanakhte had inflicted on Harker – suspending him for days just centimetres from a vat of blood – had taken his body and his mind beyond its limits. A waking nightmare of deprivation. And he simply wasn't recovering. Every day he looked a little more frail, a little older. He would forget things and always seemed as if half his mind was in another place. He was always thirsty for blood, but no amount could quench his appetite. The illness had taken hold, and was eating away at him.

"Have you talked to him about the Foundation again?" asked Luke.

"He refuses to go," said Evelyn. "Says he knows he'll get better. I think he's avoiding it, though – he's too proud to ask for their help."

The Stein Foundation was Victor Frankenstein's legacy to the world: a privately funded medical research centre based in Devon, built on the site of family property, where Luke had spent a number of family holidays. His father had set it up when Luke was little, but over the decades it seemed it had grown into a wealthy and pioneering laboratory, developing pharmaceuticals and biotech.

Harker had told him that most of the Foundation were simply brilliant scientists in their fields, and only the Board of three members, on which he sat, knew of the Immortals. They'd provided a great deal of technical help leading to Luke's reanimation after over a hundred and fifty years, and developed much of the Immortals' weapon technology.

As Luke and Evelyn walked slowly behind the cathedral, a thought occurred to him.

"Maybe we can kill two birds with one stone," he said.

"Huh?" said Evelyn.

"Persuade your dad that we need the Foundation's help with the werewolves, but then get them to look into curing him too."

"He'll probably see through it," said Evelyn.

"Got to be worth a try, though?"

Evelyn managed a smile. "You might be right. Thanks, Luke."

The other Immortals were standing beside the angel tomb, where a secret elevator would take them down into the base in the old crypt. But when Luke caught up he saw that something was wrong. No one was moving into the tomb's entrance. Dodger's head was flicking around, and Harker stood straighter than normal. Above, Raziel hunched on a flying buttress.

"What's up?" said Luke.

Aurora sniffed. "I smell something," she said, then narrowed her eyes. "There are werewolves here."

CHAPTER 4

L uke's muscles tensed, battle-ready. Aurora nodded, then kicked open the stone door. Inside the mausoleum, there was no obvious tampering with the hidden elevator.

"Are you sure?" asked Dodger. "Maybe you've just got a hair stuck up yer nose."

Aurora's gaze drilled into him. "I'm sure," she said. "They're down there. In the base."

The crypt was forty feet beneath the ground floor of the cathedral, blocked off from the public. It had been here that Victor Frankenstein had situated a secret laboratory, and the Immortals looked after it still. It had been here, too, that Luke's dead body had been reanimated after being preserved for over a century and a half in a vat of formaldehyde. *How could anyone else know about the lair?* Luke wondered uneasily. *Or the secret entrance.*

Aurora drew her Smith & Wesson, flicked open the barrel and began to load bullets into the chamber. Luke tried to keep his breathing steady and his mind clear. As Evelyn never tired of telling him, he had the advantage of several fighting uploads to his cerebral cortex – martial arts, weapons training, heightened reaction times. It was just a case of not losing his head, and accessing it all when it mattered. But that was easier said than done. Sometimes, he felt like a chef with all the right ingredients and no recipe. Dodger, meanwhile, spun two daggers in his palms. Evelyn reached into her back harness and took out her fighting staff.

Harker summoned Raziel with a flick of his wrist and the gargoyle landed outside the tomb, with a thud that Luke felt in his feet. "Let's go," Harker ordered.

They all climbed into the large elevator, Raziel last of all, stooping his folded wings through the doors.

"Luke, are you prepared?" asked Harker.

Luke lifted his right arm, and let the lightning blade extend in a curve of light from the aperture under his wrist. Among all his other enhancements and uploads, it was his favourite – a weapon he could summon with just a thought.

"I think so," he said.

The elevator descended gently and came to a halt.

As the doors opened, Luke looked out into the empty hall of the crypt. It seemed completely normal.

"Diamond formation," Harker said.

"Dad, stay in the middle," said Evelyn.

Dodger and Aurora nodded, fanning sideways. Luke took point, with Evelyn at the rear and Raziel and Harker in the centre.

The workstations and monitors were as they'd left them. The CCTV screens fed back images from around the city. The circular board table still had the pizza boxes they'd abandoned when they'd received the tip-off about the attack. Still, there was no guarantee that it was safe to walk back in here. The labs and the living quarters were all out of sight behind other doors; anyone could be hiding there.

"BIOS?" said Harker.

"Welcome back, Jonathan," said a woman's voice. The computer system that operated in the base had many functions – another benefit of having the Stein Foundation's vast resources.

"Security update, please," said Harker.

"All security measures intact," said BIOS.

Harker frowned. "False alarm, Aurora," he said.

But Luke could see from the way Aurora covered the room with cautious footsteps that she wasn't satisfied.

"The pepperoni's mine," said Dodger. He slipped his daggers out of sight in a fluid motion, then sat down on the edge of the table and reached for a cold slice of pizza. Evelyn harnessed her weapon again, and Luke let his blade retract. He dropped his satchel by the table.

"I'll be outside," said Raziel, backing into the elevator again. When he wasn't on active missions, he tended to rest among the cathedral's spires, out of sight, but always on guard. It wasn't like he needed to keep warm, or even eat, like the rest of them.

The door swished close, and the elevator's hum faded out of earshot. Luke began to remove his scrapbook from his bag when he sensed a movement and his head snapped up.

A creature covered in thick pale fur stepped out from behind a column, and Luke's blade shot out without him even having to send it a command. "Company!" he said.

Aurora raised her gun, and a slice of pizza dropped from Dodger's lips.

More werewolves emerged from hiding, unfolding out from behind the room's supporting pillars. Luke counted eight of them. Like all of their kind when transformed, they were neither wolf nor person, but huge, lithe, hairy creatures stalking on powerful hind legs. Their forelegs hung almost to the ground, ending in long claws. Eyes flashed yellow over wrinkled muzzles, and their mouths glistened with jagged teeth. Luke shuddered.

"Why didn't BIOS pick them up?" said Dodger, drawing his daggers.

"We can worry about that later," said Evelyn.

"So much for state-of-the-art," grumbled Dodger.

Luke was more concerned about the fact that the

werewolves weren't in human form. Like Aurora had said in the alley, the lunar conditions were all wrong.

"What are you doing here?" asked Harker.

The werewolves didn't speak, but that was hardly surprising. Luke knew full well from his studies in werewolf anatomy that their human vocal cords didn't survive the transformation. The creatures seemed completely focused as they moved into a semicircle, surrounding the Immortals, their claws rattling lightly on the polished concrete floor. A growl came from the tallest creature, the one with pale fur, and the wolves began to stalk forward slowly. It was clearly the leader.

"Tanner?" said Aurora, her barrel swinging to face the pale werewolf.

"Friend of yours?" said Evelyn, withdrawing her staff and twirling the fighting pole. Its metal extensions snapped out, and gleamed in the crypt's spotlights.

The pale werewolf took another step closer, crouching on its back legs.

"I'll shoot, Tanner," said Aurora. "Don't do anything dumb."

The werewolf pounced, flying through the air. At the same time the Smith & Wesson exploded and the creature stopped dead in the air and fell to the ground. Before Luke's eyes, it changed. Every sinew seemed to spasm as its torso shrank. Long limbs retracted into their sockets and the hair all over its body withered away. A man dressed in leathers lay on the floor, completely still. His jacket fell open to reveal a bloody mess where the gunshot had hit him.

"He won't be down long," said Aurora.

The remaining werewolves howled, then attacked as one. Evelyn stepped in front of her father, and met a bulky darker werewolf with a blow to its head that sent it reeling. Luke saw something glint on the back of its neck as it fell.

Two wolves leapt towards Luke. The ocular lens slowed their path through the air to half-speed. The first werewolf raked its claws at his face. Luke judo rolled, ducking the swipe and avoiding the snapping jaws of the second werewolf attacking from the flank. He swiped his lightning blade in a downwards slice, leaving a cauterised gash down the second werewolf's side. The smell of burned hair was disgusting. Luke spun back to the first creature. Too late. A paw cuffed the side of his head, throwing him sideways with incredible force. He heard Aurora's gun go off again, but then a ricochet.

Luke staggered to his knees in a desperate attempt to defend himself. A foot shoved him in the chest, pinning him to the floor. Drool spilled over his face as the werewolf leaned down, jaws open wide. Hot, putrid breath washed over him. He tried to swing his arm, but the creature held him down.

Luke's body was racked with terror. *This isn't going to end well.*

Dodger shot past, dagger blade flashing. Luke heard the elevator doors again. He saw the teeth come towards his face – horrifyingly slowly, thanks to his lens implant.

Great! Eaten in slow motion ...

And then the werewolf was gone, whipped away in a blur of grey. Luke sat up to see Raziel carrying the creature high towards the hall's lofty ceiling. He threw it against a wall with bone-crunching force.

While the others fought, Harker had a werewolf stalking towards him. He lifted his cane and Luke heard it thrum. The werewolf in front of him jerked back. Harker fired again, knocking it off its feet. Luke hadn't even realised the cane was a weapon. But though energy bolts were good for crowd control, they weren't going to stop two hundred kilos of angry werewolf. The creature righted itself, and the next shot barely slowed it down. It slammed into Harker and began to tear at his chest with its claws. Blood spattered the walls.

"Dad!" cried Evelyn. She was up against two herself, just about keeping them at bay. Dodger appeared in a series of flashes behind one, daggers glinting as he stabbed and stabbed. The werewolf flailed to catch him, missing every time.

Luke sprang up and ran towards Harker. He vaulted over a werewolf and threw himself through the air, burying his blade in the back of the one attacking Harker.

It howled and fell to the side. A time-saver only – without silver, the injury wouldn't be permanent. Harker's front was covered in blood, but he was breathing.

The werewolf Raziel had broken was already on its feet, one long paw hanging limp. The one called Tanner was finding his feet, the injury in his chest clotted and beginning to seal. Luke saw Raziel himself had three creatures hanging off his wings. They raked and gouged relentlessly with their claws and teeth, raining chips of stone across the ground.

Aurora's gun came spinning past him on the ground – she was locked in battle with another, her hands gripping its paws as it pinned her down. She headbutted the creature in the nose and managed to roll on top of it. "What do you want?" she shouted.

The werewolf was getting the better of her, rolling her over. Luke brought the gun to bear. He saw Aurora's eyes widen. "Hey, kid! Don't point that thing at—"

Luke pulled the trigger and the werewolf sagged on top of her. Aurora's face went from shocked to angry to disbelieving in less than a second.

"Thank me later," he said.

She heaved the werewolf's bulk off her, but the other lycanthropes headed her way. Raziel hurtled downwards, out of control, two wolves raking at his back, another biting his throat. They leapt off just before the gargoyle smashed into a bench of computers. The three wolves left him lying there and joined the ones stalking Aurora.

Luke realised something. *Whatever this is*, he thought, *it's about her . . .*

"We need to get out of here," said Evelyn, crouched over her dad. "There are too many of them."

In a blur, Dodger zipped between several of the approaching werewolves, and began to hit buttons on a console.

"Flight room's activated," he said. "Let's go!"

On the far side of the room, a staircase extended from the ceiling just as Luke downed another werewolf with the pistol. He tried to cock the hammer again, but the chamber was empty.

Raziel picked himself up weakly and began to run in lumbering steps at the werewolves crowding around Aurora. He smashed through them like a bowling ball. The werewolves crashed to the floor, several with twisted limbs and broken bones. But one by one they found their feet again. Luke swallowed as their legs snapped back into position under their fur. *This is hopeless. We're fighting a losing battle.*

"Let's go!" he said.

"Leave me," said Harker as Evelyn placed her hands beneath him. "I'm finished."

Luke watched her lift her father easily. Her strength was roughly three times that of a normal thirteen-year-old human girl. Even so, Harker had lost so much weight since the ordeal with Sanakhte, a normal thirteen-year-old probably could have lifted him too.

As the werewolves continued to heal themselves, Evelyn carried her father to the stairs. Dodger was waiting by the bottom. "Luke? Get a shift on!" he shouted.

But Aurora was still in trouble, surrounded. Luke slipped the Smith & Wesson in his satchel and fired up the lightning blade. He didn't need to take them all on – just create an escape route. Then he remembered he had a UV grenade in his pocket. That would have to do.

"Hey, howlers!" he cried, popping the pin. They all turned. "Catch!"

Luke tossed the grenade into the middle of them, and Aurora dived behind a bank of monitors. The explosion ripped through the room. Unlike a traditional hand grenade, UV grenades weren't designed to throw out shrapnel. Their power was percussive – displacing anything in the immediate vicinity of the blast. In this case, that meant chucking the werewolves and the consoles in every direction. Luke plunged through the smoke and found Aurora half-sitting. She was covered in dust, barely conscious. He grabbed one arm and heaved, but barely moved her. "Come on!" he said.

Dodger arrived too and gripped her other arm. "Up you get, whiskers."

"Don't call me that," Aurora growled, getting to her feet

unsteadily. Luke and Dodger helped her hobble past the stirring bodies and through the door where Raziel waited.

"I'll stall them," said the gargoyle. He threw up a wing, completely blocking the door. Straight away, his stone body juddered as the snarling werewolves threw themselves against the barrier. "You should get to the helicopter, Master Frankenstein," he said calmly. "I can't hold them for long."

Luke didn't need telling twice. He ran up to the flight platform where the Immortals' helicopter was waiting. Evelyn, who had been completing her piloting training with Luke, jumped into the pilot seat and flicked switches, starting the rotors. The platform rose and a section of roof opened like petals in a flower, revealing a black starlit sky. The exit was a small piece of waste garden in the cathedral grounds. From the air, it looked completely unremarkable, surrounded on all sides by crumbling walls – a perfect launch pad.

"Where's Raziel?" she said, as Luke hopped in the back beside Dodger. Harker was lying opposite them, his head resting in Aurora's lap. Evelyn's father's eyelids were fluttering. Luke wondered how much blood he'd lost.

"He'll come," said Dodger. "He's got wings, remember."

Evelyn eased the chopper off the pad. A booming sound made Luke look down, to where Raziel was clawing his way up the steps, trying to get airborne while a werewolf hung off one wing.

"Go! Go!" said Dodger.

Two more werewolves scrambled past Raziel and hurled themselves, bodies stretching, at the helicopter. One caught the rail, and the other landed with a thump on the front windshield. Its saliva streaked the viewing glass as its teeth raked down.

"I just cleaned that," muttered Dodger.

Luke watched the other hang on as the helicopter rose into the night air. He leant outside the open door and sliced with the lightning blade, severing both hairy paws. The werewolf dropped thirty metres and landed in a heap on the helipad. Evelyn nosed the chopper over the cathedral as the one remaining werewolf gripped the front like a limpet.

"Any idea what we do about this one?" she asked. "He seems determined."

The answer came a moment later when Raziel appeared, flying at their side. He veered ahead, burying stone claws into the werewolf's fur and ripping him off the helicopter's windshield. Luke watched the creature squirm in the gargoyle's grip as it was carried over the river, then dropped. He didn't see the splash.

"Well," said Dodger. "*That* was fun."

"Luke, take the controls," said Evelyn.

"Now?" he said. He had flown the chopper before, but it didn't stop the anxiety fluttering in his chest.

"Use your upload," she said. "Just concentrate, Luke. I need to look after my dad."

She was already clambering out of the seat, so he didn't really have a choice. He scrambled past into the pilot's seat and found the pedals with his feet, gripping the stick. *I can do this.*

Evelyn climbed into the back beside Harker, and took down the first-aid kit from its cabin compartment. Meanwhile Luke worked on keeping the chopper steady, eyes skipping over the banks of controls. Gradually, like a picture resolving into focus, he identified the myriad dials and displays. Altimeter, blade rpm, headlights, wipers, GPS. He flicked his eyes to the sky ahead, and the *whoop-whoop* of the blades became the only sound.

Raziel glided about fifty metres away on the port side. He seemed no worse for wear after the fight, aside from a few chips to his craggy face and the tip of one wing missing. Luke knew the gargoyle felt pain, but still had little idea about Raziel's physiology, despite pestering Raziel to tell him. Dodger claimed that the secretive way the gargoyle carved himself new flesh from stone was magic, but Luke, like his dad, was a scientist. He wanted to understand it properly and document it.

"How's he doing?" said Aurora from the back.

Luke looked over his shoulder. She was sitting up, craning her neck, and peering at Harker.

"The cuts are quite deep," said Evelyn, her face taut. Luke

48

saw she'd put some dressings over the wounds. "His heart rate's slow." She touched her father's cheek. "Dad?"

Luke faced forward again. Vampires were tough creatures – tougher than the stories made out. Daylight burned them nastily. But holy water, crosses, garlic … useless. The only sure-fire ways to take out a healthy blood-sucker were a stake, decapitation, or exsanguination – severe blood loss.

Harker wasn't healthy, though. He was already weak. Luke had no idea if he could pull through. The thought made Luke's chest tighten. What would Evelyn do if Harker didn't make it? How would she cope? They were so close. Harker's wife and son had been killed by vampire attackers, but Evelyn had survived, cursed too with the vampire gene. She and her father had comforted each other through their grief, growing only closer as the decades passed.

"So, where to?" asked Aurora.

Luke accessed the mapping systems on the helicopter display and set a course. The base was compromised – no going back there. And they couldn't land in Greater London without arousing attention. A red dot flashed 217 miles west, in the middle of Dartmoor. It was a place he hadn't been since he was eight years old, five years ago. Or around a hundred and sixty years ago, depending on how you counted.

"The Stein Foundation," he said.

"How long will it take?" said Evelyn.

Luke did the mental calculation. "A couple of hours max."

"I don't get it," said Dodger. "What did they want? And how come they were in wolf form?"

"I saw something on their heads," said Evelyn. "Something metal."

"Me too," said Luke. "Aurora – you knew them?"

"Some of them," said Aurora. "From a long time ago – another world."

"You must have done something to really annoy them," said Dodger.

Aurora shook her head. "That's the thing – I didn't. They were my pack. Back in the States." She paused. "My friends."

"I'd hate to see how they treat their enemies," said Dodger.

"Just shut your mouth, kid," said Aurora. "I'm thinking."

Dodger seemed to know when to take a hint, because he didn't say another word.

"This must be connected to the *canes umbrarum* killing," said Luke. "Maybe the American wolves are trying to take over territory."

"I don't buy it," said Aurora thoughtfully. "There's plenty of space back home."

"It can't be a coincidence that there are suddenly werewolves running riot in London," said Evelyn.

"No, it can't," said Harker weakly.

Luke was glad to hear his voice again. "Dad, just rest," said Evelyn.

But Luke saw Harker sitting up in the pilot's mirror. His wounds still looked raw, the cuts leaking blood. Normally a vampire would have healed by now. "The Stein Foundation can help," he said.

"That's good," said Luke. He flicked on the communications switch. "Shall I radio ahead?"

Harker paused for a moment before replying. "No, let's surprise them."

Luke caught a slightly odd tone in the vampire's voice, but a beeping from the console interrupted his thoughts.

"It's a radio signal," said Evelyn. She reached across and flicked a switch.

"... *yourself. I repeat, this is Heathrow Air Traffic Control, and you are flying in regulated airspace. Please identify yourself. Over.*"

Luke groaned. "What do I say?" he asked.

"How should I know?" said Evelyn. "Can't you just fly out of their airspace again? Maybe they won't care."

"OK," said Luke. His eyes searched the ground below. Sure enough, among the suburbs, he saw the parallel lines of lights marking a distant runway. He banked the helicopter away.

"*Unidentified craft, you have entered regulated—*"

Dodger switched off the radio with a grin. "Problem solved."

"Let's hope so," said Harker. He stroked a hand through his hair. "I wanted to say. The Stein Foundation has changed a lot since Victor's day. The division which deals with us – the Special Research department – is just a small part."

"It's still in that old mansion, isn't it?" asked Dodger. Harker nodded.

"My mum's family's house," said Luke. The memories surfaced with surprising clarity. Sunny days fishing in a pond, his aunt laying out food on a blanket. His dad flying a kite across the moors. Happy thoughts. But as the images melted away, Luke felt a pang of loss stab at his chest, and his breath shuddered. Everything had changed now. Everyone he remembered at the Dartmoor house – his aunts and cousins, his father – were all gone. He was the only one left. Luke felt a lump in his throat, and he realised how hard it was going to be returning there. *I have to focus.* He blinked and tried to gather himself together. The city of London was relying on him – and Harker was as well. He didn't think he could cope with losing him, too.

Dodger's voice snapped Luke's attention back. "So if Victor set it up," Dodger said to Luke, "and it's his old house, I guess that makes you the boss. Rightful heir and all that?"

Luke frowned. Put like that, it sounded sort of reasonable, but a little bit daunting. What did he know about running a Foundation?

"I'm sure it's not that simple," said Evelyn, glancing at Luke, her brow furrowed.

Raziel suddenly appeared on the port side, flying close. "Master Luke!" he called.

"Uh-oh," said Dodger. "Four o'clock."

Luke looked over his right shoulder and his heart sank. Another helicopter flew in their wake, closing from two hundred metres. His mental directory identified it as a Merlin HC3. He spotted at least one mounted machine gun. He wondered if it had any air-to-air ordinance.

"Raziel, go to altitude and stay out of sight," he said, picked up by the gargoyle through his earpiece.

As Raziel climbed away, the console beeped and Luke switched the receiver on.

"*Unidentified craft, we have been dispatched to escort you for landing. Failure to comply will result in countermeasures. Please adjust your course and fall in . . .*"

"I don't like the sound of *countermeasures*," said Luke.

"I hope you're not going to do what they say," said Evelyn.

"No way," Luke replied. Leaving aside that he was a thirteen-year-old piloting a top-secret helicopter without a licence, he really wasn't sure the authorities would accept four passengers consisting of two vampires (one half-dead), a werewolf, and a bewitched street urchin. Not a lot of choice, really.

"Strap in, team," he said, "and prepare for evasive manoeuvres."

CHAPTER 5

L uke jammed the stick forward, and the chopper lurched. In the back, Dodger moaned. "You know I get airsick!"

In the mirror, the Merlin banked after them. It wasn't as manoeuvrable as the Immortals' helicopter, but Luke knew it was first-class military hardware with a higher top speed and longer range.

"Can't we shoot 'em down?" said Dodger. "This contraption's got guns or lasers, hasn't it?"

"I don't think it's got lasers," said Luke. Weapons-wise, they were actually about even. "Anyway, I'm not going to deploy missiles against innocent pilots."

"Must be hard having a conscience," muttered Dodger.

Luke steered south-east, climbing and trying to keep calm. "Maybe they'll lose interest once we're out of 'secured airspace'."

"Nope – still with us," said Evelyn. She arched an eyebrow at Luke. "Is that the best you can do?"

Luke couldn't resist a challenge. He pulled back on the lever, and the chopper's nose rose sharply. They shot upwards on a steep trajectory.

"Go easy," said Dodger. "Seriously, I'm gonna chuck."

"If you're sick on me, I'll chuck *you* out," said Aurora. Luke saw she was gripping the side of her seat tightly.

The helicopter juddered a little as they entered clouds at four thousand metres. Luke maintained his course, flying blind, then flicked on the radar. For a moment he thought he'd lost their tail, then a red dot started pinging and the radio crackled again.

"*. . . unidentified craft, this is RAF Middlesex. Change course or we will open fire. This is your last warning.*"

"They're probably bluffing," said Evelyn.

The clouds cleared around them and Luke saw empty fields below. If they went down here, there'd be no civilian casualties. "I don't think they—" Luke began.

The alarms on the console flashed and squeaked. "Incoming!" said Evelyn.

Luke dragged the lever sideways as a missile streaked past the left rung and disappeared on a trail of smoke.

"As I was saying," said Luke, gritting his teeth with his heart pounding, as he pulled the chopper into a steep climb, "I think they might be serious."

Phut–phut–phut.

Luke ducked at the sound, terrifyingly close to his head. He glanced in both mirrors but lost the Merlin.

"Machine gun," said Aurora. She pulled a lever and their own mounted gun popped up from the fuselage. Aurora spun it around. "Where the hell are they?" she muttered.

"Hold your fire," said Luke. "They're Her Majesty's armed forces!"

"I'm American," said Aurora.

Luke heard the Merlin's rotors and jerked his head around. He saw it coming at them from ninety degrees, cutting through cloud. The muzzle-flashes reached him before the sound. Luke tried to swerve, then the chopper shook as rounds impacted with the side.

"Just shoot the thing," said Dodger. "Lasers, bullets, arrows – I don't care!"

"No!" said Evelyn. "Luke, get us out of here."

Luke scanned the alarm systems. By sheer fluke, their engines still hadn't been hit, but they couldn't ride their luck for ever if they refused to fire back. *Time for something special.*

"Hold on, everyone!" He killed the rotors.

"What are you going to—" Dodger screamed as the chopper plummeted, and Aurora let out a cry.

Luke's heart bobbed up into his throat as he watched

the altimeter reading dropping in a blur: 3000, 2800, 2500, 2000 . . .

His body wanted to leave his seat but his belt kept him fastened in. 1500, 1000, 500 . . .

Several instruments were talking to him calmly, but the essence of each message was the same: *You are about to die.*

"Luke, we'll crash!" said Evelyn.

"No we won't!" he shouted back.

At least I hope not . . .

Holding his breath, he ramped the rotors gently into motion. Too much and the forces would just snap them; too little and they wouldn't get up in time. His knuckles were white on the throttle, sensing the chopper's shuddering vibrations. He could see the ground now – pastures and trees, the odd farmhouse – rushing to meet them. He increased rotor speed, as much as he dared. *Hold her steady . . . don't panic . . .*

Their descent slowed, and the nose-end dipped, throwing him forward in his seat.

Two hundred feet. His stomach flooding with dread, Luke saw it all in slow motion. Birds flocking in panic. A cow looking up. Lights from the window of a house. A car skidding as the chopper's lights arced across its headlights.

One hundred feet from the ground and the weight of the chopper still moved agonisingly downward towards a field. *We're not going to make it . . .* With a jolt of horror, the memory of falling to his death from the window of the British Museum flashed into his brain – the tumble through the cold air, the black dagger lodged to the hilt in his chest ... Terror gripped hold of him, making his muscles seize up.

Evelyn's shouts brought him to his senses. "Luke, pull up!"

He rammed the rotors to full power and the helicopter found some forward momentum at last. He gripped the lever and pulled back, as though brute strength and body weight could keep the chopper from hitting the ground. He didn't need an altimeter to tell him it was going to be very, very close.

Please ...

He closed his eyes and waiting for the unforgiving crunch of metal.

It never came.

"Woohoo!" yelled Evelyn.

Luke dared to look. Clear air, treetops, the powerful thrumming of the blades.

"You had your eyes closed!" said Dodger. "I saw!"

Luke looked back to check on his passengers. Dodger was pale, and Evelyn grinned as she leaned over her father. "Not bad," she said.

Aurora, clutching the door, gave him a small nod then looked upwards through the window. "I think we lost them."

A quick look at the radar confirmed it.

Relief surged through Luke's heart in an ecstatic rush. His palms were sweaty on the throttle and he pushed open the vents to let some of the cool night air wash over his face. The digital display chart showed them crossing the invisible border between Berkshire and Surrey. On the ground was a small river snaking blackly through rolling hills. Luke matched his flight path to the contours of the land, flying twenty metres above the landscape at a steady ninety knots. Sure, they might wake a few light sleepers, but by the time anyone peered from a window, they'd be long gone. And no radar would pick them up this low.

"Next stop, Dartmoor," said Luke.

By the time the sun rose behind them an hour later, they were flying at high altitude over the vast scrubland and heather of Dartmoor. Luke had skirted wide of Exeter airport, just in case they attracted any more unwanted attention, and the detour had added ten minutes to the journey time. It was a clear morning, the sky a vibrant blue, and Luke could see the long spit of Devon and Cornwall stretched out towards the horizon straight ahead, flanked by the Irish Sea to the north and the Atlantic on the port side.

He checked back. Evelyn was asleep, arm still draped over Harker. He was unconscious by the looks of it, and his skin was pale. *The illness is stopping him healing properly*, thought Luke. *It's draining his immortality.*

Dodger slept as well – leaning sideways, mouth gaping, against Aurora's massive shoulder. She was looking at something in her hand, staring intently. Luke remembered the pain in her face as she'd shot the one called Tanner. Strange to think of her having a pack, and friends – aside from the Immortals, he'd always known her as a loner. A vigilante dispensing justice in Victorian London. But if she'd had friends, what had made them turn against her?

When he hadn't been watching the chopper's readings, Luke had been thinking hard about the attack. Two things stood out as completely wrong. The fact they were in wolf form when the moon wasn't full, and that they'd managed to bypass BIOS. If Harker got better – *when* he did – he might have some answers.

"We're almost there," said Luke loudly. "You OK?"

Aurora looked up, then tossed her coin in the air and caught it. The movement jerked Dodger awake. "What? Where, Nancy sweetheart?" he mumbled.

"We're landing soon," said Aurora. "And don't call me Nancy."

Dodger rubbed his eyes and yawned. "I hope they've some breakfast. I'd kill for a bacon sarnie."

Luke checked the map and saw their destination flashing two miles ahead. He stared out through the windscreen at the dark and barren moorland below. It was the same as he remembered. As they flew over their destination, he searched the ground, and pointed. "Is that the Stein Foundation?"

Evelyn, who'd woken too, nodded. "That's it."

From the air, Luke saw several low-level tent-like buildings sprawled across a dip in the ground. Solar panels – hundreds of them – glinted in the first light of the sun. In the centre of it, Luke recognised the manor house made of dark stone. It seemed grimmer than in his recollection and the Land Rover parked beside it looked out of place. *What had you been expecting?* Luke said to himself. *The old coach and horses?* The single-track road, once gravel, was now plain tarmac. It snaked from the large house for miles across the landscape – still the only access road. Where the orchard used to be was what could only be a runway with a large corrugated hangar next to it. Security seemed to consist of a wire perimeter fence encircling the buildings.

"What are the tents for?" he asked.

"Agricultural projects," said Harker in the back. Luke was relieved to hear his voice, however weak it sounded. "Much of the Foundation's energy is spent looking for new ways to grow produce in a variety of inhospitable environments. The fight against food poverty."

Evelyn pointed to a patch of ground marked with a letter "H" beside the hangar.

"Put us down there," she said.

Luke swung the chopper down, and let the rungs bump the ground gently. The house was a hundred metres away, and now Luke saw it closer, it brought back a distant memory of being welcomed into the candlelit grand foyer, his father, energetic as ever, rushing off to speak with other scientists. Luke shook his head. Now wasn't the time for nostalgia.

He switched off the engines and the rotors gradually spun to a halt. He climbed out with the others. The air smelt cool and fresh.

Dodger did a few stretches. "Ah – solid ground!" he said.

Harker stepped off, leaning heavily on Aurora. The new dressings on his wounds were already stained with fresh blood. The sight caused Luke's stomach to sink with worry.

From the house strode a woman of about fifty, wearing jeans and a dark green country jacket. Her long brown hair had a few grey streaks and was tied in a ponytail. Luke was slightly alarmed to see four armed men in black fatigues flanking her. But, as she came closer, she gave them a wave and they stopped in their tracks.

"Jonathan," she said. "We weren't expecting you. Evelyn, how are you?"

"We've been better," said Evelyn. "Can we come inside?"

The woman's eyes swept over Dodger and Aurora quickly, then paused on Luke for longer. She frowned at him. "Of course," she said.

Raziel dropped from the sky, feet thumping down, and

the armed men all whipped up their guns. The gargoyle's chest was heaving, and his skin looked damp from the cold air, giving him the appearance of sweating.

The woman took a deep breath. "You must be Raziel," she said.

Raziel nodded, folding his wings. "Correct."

"Stand down," said the woman. "He's no threat – I hope."

"Dr Pavlovic," said Evelyn, taking charge. "Let me introduce the Immortals properly. You know my father already. This is indeed Raziel, and these are Aurora Cage and the Artful Dodger."

The werewolf tipped her hat a fraction, while Dodger whipped his from his head with an elaborate, courtly bow. "Don't believe what you've read in the book. Dickens was a fantasist."

"And last of all," said Evelyn, "here is Luke. Luke Frankenstein."

Luke stepped forwards and held out his hand. His father had always said a firm handshake was the start of any good friendship.

The woman held out her own. "Dr Anna Pavlovic," she said, eyes sweeping over Luke, as if examining a piece of machinery. "Welcome to the Stein Foundation."

"Pleased to be here," said Luke, shaking her hand. "I remember this place, from when I was a boy."

"You're still a boy, aren't you?" said Dr Pavlovic briskly.

"Yes, I suppose so, but—" Luke's tongue got stuck. "What I meant was—"

"Don't worry, I understand," said Dr Pavlovic. "Come, let me show you inside."

The security detail watched open-mouthed as Raziel strode past them. Aurora helped Evelyn support Harker.

"Is he all right?" asked Dr Pavlovic, pausing.

"Had a barney with a pack of werewolves," said Dodger. "Looks better than some of them."

"I thought vamp— I thought his kind couldn't get ill."

Luke frowned. He wondered if the doctor knew anything at all about the fight with Sanakhte and what Harker and the rest of them had undergone. "It's a long story," he said weakly.

Harker let out a moan, and Evelyn held him up. "Can we please go inside?" she said.

"Of course," said the doctor.

They reached the door and, as it opened automatically, Luke had a sudden and strong vision of the space he was about to walk into. He remembered the boot room, then the pantry, leading to the huge stone-flagged kitchen ...

But it wasn't like that at all now.

Most of the walls had been ripped out, and the interior was painted white, giving everything a sterile sheen. There were offices behind glass partitions, and lots of sleek computers on desks. The change was a shock, and made him feel disorientated for a second.

The security remained outside.

"Privacy," said Dr Pavlovic, loudly and firmly. In an instant, the glass darkened, and she led them along a series of white corridors. Luke realised they followed the old layout of the house and, with a sudden jolt, he worked out where they were. The passageway to the dining room. Echoes of long dead voices met his ears – his father calling for him to recite anatomy for guests. The laughter accompanied by the chink of glasses. The hushed and excited voices of his father and the other scientists, late at night. The scolding of his nanny, when Luke was discovered eavesdropping . . .

"Please keep up," said Dr Pavlovic over her shoulder. Luke realised he had fallen back, and hurried after the others. It was strange, feeling like a visitor in a place that had been so familiar to him. They reached an office, which had been the old butler's pantry. The plaque on the door read "Dr Anna Pavlovic, Managing Director". She stood aside, smiling politely as they paraded in. Her room had a large desk, with two flat-screen monitors. Several wall-mounted screens showed scenery from around the world in such high definition it was like looking out of a window on to the real thing. In glass cases mounted on the walls were a mixture of scientific equipment and specimen displays. A robotic forearm, a large 3D model of a human eye, some sort of organ that might have been a heart sliced in cross section and preserved in fluid. The wall behind the desk was entirely shelved with hundreds of books and journals. Luke felt slightly better, seeing the evidence of scientific research – it was what his father would have wanted.

As the door closed behind them, Dr Pavlovic's smile fell away.

"Mr Harker, what on earth are you doing here, turning up unannounced? I thought we had an agreement."

Harker looked ready to drop, but his face stiffened at her tone. "We had no other choice," he said, then began to cough, a horrible hacking sound. He reached in his pocket and found a handkerchief. When he withdrew it from his mouth, it was bloody. Dr Pavlovic's eyebrows rose, but apart from that she didn't even flinch. Luke felt a stab of annoyance.

Evelyn lowered her dad into a chair. "Can't you see he needs medical attention?" she said. "He's on the Board here, so you've got to help him. You know he can't be admitted to a normal hospital."

"Very well," said Dr Pavlovic, her face cold. She spoke to no one in particular. "Intercom, medical. I need an infirmary team for our guest. Records under *Harker, Dr Jonathan.*"

"Thank you," said Evelyn, glowering.

"Our Southwark base was attacked," Luke explained.

"Werewolves, you said," said Dr Pavlovic. Her mouth twisted in distaste. "I'm afraid it's not my area of expertise.

I'm a medical doctor, you see. I'm interested in treating people with illnesses, not lycanthropy."

Luke was starting to really dislike Dr Pavlovic. Who did she think she was? They were interrupted by the door opening and three doctors in white coats entered, pushing a stretcher. Harker, with Evelyn's help, lay down gently. "We'll get you well soon, Dad," she said.

As the doctors began to wheel Harker away, Evelyn took a few steps after him.

"He'll be well looked after," said Dr Pavlovic.

"Will he?" snapped Evelyn. "Because so far it looks very much like you don't want us here."

"I apologise if I've given you that impression, Miss Harker," said Dr Pavlovic. She tapped a few times on her keyboard. "I'm just a little surprised by your arrival, that's all. Most of the staff here know little or nothing of your group, and anything that jeopardises the Foundation's operations troubles me greatly."

Luke was taken aback. He had assumed they would be welcomed at the Foundation, but it was clearly the opposite. No wonder Harker was hesitant about coming here.

"We're not jeopardising anything," said Evelyn. "And you better get used to us – we're going to be here a while."

"I'm sorry?" said Dr Pavlovic.

Luke was riled up, but he took a deep breath and forced himself to calm down. Arguing wouldn't help anyone. "What Evelyn means," said Luke, "is that we'll need to base ourselves here – as I said, the crypt has been compromised."

"Base yourselves here?" said Dr Pavlovic. "I'm afraid that won't be possible. We're a scientific research facility, not a . . . not a . . . " She looked at each of them, as if searching for a way to describe the Immortals.

Evelyn slammed a hand down on the desk. "Let me make it easy for you," she said acidly. "This is Luke's house. This whole place belongs to Luke. You are employed by Luke. And we – *Doctor* – are staying. Got it?"

Dodger sucked in a breath. "Anyone else picking up a slightly uncomfortable vibe?" Everyone stared at him. "I'll shut up," he muttered.

Dr Pavlovic shot Luke a glance. "Very well," she said. "I think I understand."

There was a knock at the door.

Dr Pavlovic pressed a button on her desk, and the door became transparent. On the other side stood a tall, straight-backed man, with a bald head. He wore dark corduroy trousers and a white shirt open at the neck with rolled-up sleeves. A pair of lightweight wire-framed spectacles sat on his nose.

"Enter," said Dr Pavlovic.

The door slid across and the man did a double take. "Oh my, would you look at that?" he said. American accent,

Luke thought. The man walked in cautiously, right up to Raziel, completely unafraid, then took off his glasses and held up a hand. "May I touch you?" he asked.

Raziel shifted awkwardly. "You may."

The man ran his fingers across the stone of Raziel's wing. "Incredible!" he said. "It's one thing reading about it, of course, but another thing entirely to see you in person." Then his eyes passed over Evelyn, and Dodger, before coming to rest on Aurora. "And you must be Aurora Cage."

"How d'you know that?" asked Aurora, nostrils flaring slightly.

The bald man spun on his heels, and focused on Luke. He shook his head in wonder. "Remarkable! Harker only went and did it. I recognise you from the pictures, Luke."

Luke was about to ask what pictures, but Dodger cut in. "And who might you be, mate?"

The man slipped the glasses back. "Apologies, my friends, how rude of me. When I heard you'd arrived, I dropped what I was doing. My name is Dr Fontaine – I'm a scientist here. But you can call me Greg."

"Dr Fontaine has taken over the Immortals programme, after Dr Harker *insisted* it be restarted a year ago," said Dr Pavlovic.

"And until today, it was all just theory," said Dr Fontaine. "To see you all here, like this, is rather a shock. A pleasant one, I should add." He frowned. "And where is Jonathan?

I haven't seen him in months. Though I'm sure you've all been busy."

"In the infirmary," said Luke. "He's still weak from prolonged thirst and a werewolf attack."

"Werewolves, you say?" said Fontaine, eyes widening. "Is he all right?"

"He will be," said Evelyn, nodding as if trying to convince herself.

Dr Fontaine didn't seem to pick up on the tension in her face. "Well, that's great. And if it's werewolves that are the problem, I may have just the thing – we've been developing many new weapons, and I have one or two specifically designed to deal with such creatures."

"Not cheaply made, either," said Dr Pavlovic. "Dr Fontaine's programmes are sucking up the annual budget of the Foundation. We've already had to close down one of the genetic modification projects."

Dr Fontaine smiled awkwardly. "There's little literature to fall back on," he said. "Books written in the 1700s about werewolves contain more magic than real science. We're having to do a lot of the research from scratch." He clicked his fingers, then pointed to Aurora. "Actually, your presence will be infinitely useful, Ms Cage."

"You're not experimenting on me," said Aurora.

"They'd probably shave all your hair off," chuckled Dodger.

Dr Fontaine looked aghast. "Of course not. But—"

"No buts," said Aurora, straightening so she stood even taller. Dr Fontaine paled.

"I'd like to see what you have already on the werewolves," said Luke.

The doctor nodded. "It would be a pleasure."

"Perhaps you could show our ... guests ... to the living quarters too?" said Dr Pavlovic with what looked to Luke like a fleeting sneer. "We really can't have them running around the Foundation, scaring the staff."

Dr Fontaine clapped his hands together. "Indeed. Come with me."

As he turned and they followed him from the room, Luke felt Dr Pavlovic's icy stare on his back. What was her problem? This place wouldn't even be here if it weren't for his dad.

Dr Fontaine talked as he led them through the house, using a fingerprint recognition pad to pass through several doors along more sterile white corridors. Luke could feel his nostalgia fall away now they were focused on their mission. "Much of the facilities are actually underground," he said. "Helps to regulate temperature, and it's more secure. We must have security passes made for you too."

Dr Fontaine seemed pretty cool to Luke – a scientist a lot like his dad had been, optimistic, enthusiastic, fun. White-coated scientists were working in several sterile-looking rooms, and peered at the Immortals curiously.

"Don't worry about them," said Dr Fontaine. "All staff here have signed a non-disclosure agreement because of the sensitivity of the research. By the way, I've had your helicopter moved into the hangar – your little chase near London made the evening news."

"How did you pilot it?" said Evelyn.

Dr Fontaine laughed. "My dear girl, I designed it."

Evelyn blushed, and Luke gave her a playful shove as they reached another door.

When this one opened, Luke's feet stalled. On the other side it was a different world. This section of the house hadn't changed at all, and Luke suffered an almost physical jolt of memory as he looked up the grand staircase – wide, carpeted and old fashioned – sweeping to the upper floor.

"You OK?" asked Evelyn.

Luke nodded slowly. "I remember this part," he mumbled. Even the smell – a mixture of slight mustiness, old coal smoke and wood polish – made his heart lift yet ache with loss at the same time. He closed his eyes for a moment, and he was back there, his father waiting at the bottom of the stairs as he slid down the banister.

"Upstairs we haven't touched," said Dr Fontaine. "There are several bedrooms ... "

But Luke was already rushing up the stairs, eyes hungry as the recollections strengthened. He rounded the top and found himself in the long gallery, with doors coming off either side. His feet took him of their own accord to one in particular. He had to see if it was still here, still the same.

He twisted the knob, eased the door open, and let the past flood over him. The mahogany and leather desk, the shelves, the chaise longue where his father would sometimes drop off to sleep with a book across his chest . . .

Victor Frankenstein's study.

CHAPTER 6

"I can't believe it," said Luke. "It's just the same."

Dr Fontaine appeared at his side. "It wasn't when I arrived," he said. "They'd moved the contents into storage. I recreated it, from an old photograph. You must understand, Luke – I didn't want to be presumptuous. This is all your property, really, but it looked unlikely at the time that you would ever come back."

Luke didn't know whether to be angry, or thankful. He walked in, fingers brushing a globe on the desk, turning it on its axis. There was even a quill and inkwell. "Why did you do it?"

"Your father was a hero of mine," said Dr Fontaine softly. "It's a bit embarrassing really, but sometimes, when I'm struggling with a problem I'll come up here to think."

Luke looked at the leather-bound tomes on the shelves. Anatomy, chemistry, physics, the occult. Works of literature, too. As he rounded the desk, he saw two small pictures – pencil drawings. His mother in one, smiling serenely, and one of Luke aged six or seven in a smart buttoned jacket. Luke fought back the emotion swelling in his chest. *Did he really have to put up the pictures?* It was like Luke's memories had been taken from his head and planted in the real world.

He opened one of the drawers, and saw sheaves of papers covered in mechanical drawings. It was as if his dad had been in this very room, working, just a few hours before.

Luke felt tears threatening to fall. In a mirror he saw Evelyn hesitating on the threshold, and the others behind her.

"You can come in," he said quietly.

"Nice pad," mumbled Dodger, nodding. "Very retro."

"It reminds me of Victor," said Aurora warmly.

Evelyn took a few quick glances around, then turned. "Let's check out the weapons," she said over her shoulder.

Luke could have stayed longer, but Evelyn was right to be impatient. They weren't here for a trip down memory lane. *I need to stay focused on the mission.*

After they'd been quickly shown their bedrooms, Dr Fontaine led them back to the ground floor, then to an elevator. It whisked them down two storeys into the labs. As the doors opened, Luke looked out on to darkness.

"BIOS, lights," said Dr Fontaine.

Strip lighting flicked on sequentially to illuminate a vast open-plan space lined with wall-mounted containers in gleaming steel, and workbenches with equipment. It looked like something between a laboratory and a metal shop. At the far end was a section with several targets shaped like human silhouettes. *Firing range*, thought Luke, heart speeding up.

"BIOS, display AWWs," said Dr Fontaine. Evelyn frowned. "Anti-Werewolf Weaponry," the doctor added.

"You have BIOS here too?" she asked. Now Dr Fontaine blushed. "Let me guess – you invented that too."

The scientist gave a modest bow. Luke was impressed.

Several of the metal containers hummed into life, opening up to reveal an assortment of weapons, from things that looked like guns, to silver throwing stars and knives. Luke recognised on a digital diagnostic display something that looked like his own arm graft.

"What do you think?" asked Dr Fontaine.

"Cool!" said Luke.

Aurora picked up one of several spherical objects. "Are these grenades?" she asked.

"Stickies," said Dr Fontaine. "Filled with a highly adhesive expanding foam. The US federal authorities were developing them for dealing with prison riots. We've significantly improved the design."

Dodger went straight to a short-barrelled launcher and hoisted it off its stand. "What does this one do?"

"Erm ... I don't think you—" said Evelyn.

Dodger aimed at one of the targets and pulled the trigger. A net shot out and enveloped the mannequin.

"High-tensile flexible alloy – ninety per cent silver," said Dr Fontaine nervously, taking the gun off Dodger. "Should hold a werewolf. But if they struggle—" he turned a dial on the gun's side, and blue sparks crackled along the net's strands "—delivers up to one thousand volts."

One plinth held something that looked like a black cricket ball, with a raised seam around its equator. Luke picked it up and tossed it from hand to hand. "I had a mean leg-spin at school."

"That's a sonic grenade," said Fontaine. "Emits a high-frequency burst that should immobilise a werewolf for at least ten to fifteen seconds."

"Then what?" said Aurora. "Sing it a lullaby and send it off to sleep?"

Dr Fontaine looked puzzled rather than offended.

"Ignore her," said Dodger. "She's just grouchy."

With a *snick*ing sound, Evelyn extended her staff. Hanging from several pegs were a number of attachments. Spikes of various lengths and shapes. She screwed on a hook and spun the staff.

"You approve?" said Fontaine.

Evelyn did a backflip, and the hook arced round in a blur. "Nice," she said.

"They were your father's idea," said Dr Fontaine enthusiastically.

Evelyn paused and lowered the weapon. She stood, staring at the staff.

"He'll be OK," said Luke, coming over and resting a hand on her shoulder.

Evelyn nodded. "I know."

A number of vials on a shelf caught Luke's eye. "And what are these?"

"For Mr Dodger," said Dr Fontaine. "Silver fluoride in liquid form. The vapour will disorientate. Ingested, it has the potential to kill werewolves outright."

"Have you actually tested any of this on a live subject?" Aurora growled.

"No," said Dr Fontaine, spreading his hands. "We haven't had that opportunity."

"Then it's all theoretical," said Aurora. She held up her fists. "I think I'll take my chances with these."

Luke wasn't surprised she was prickly. Half this room seemed designed to kill her kind – though Luke knew Aurora herself was immune to silver, as the trace of the silver bullet that scarred her cheek protected her like a vaccine. But it brought to his mind another question.

"Back in London," he said, "the werewolves that attacked us were in lupine form, even though it wasn't a full moon. How's that possible?"

Dr Fontaine looked intrigued. "Interesting you should say that, and that's why I'm glad we have Miss Cage here to help us with our research." Aurora bristled, but Dr Fontaine didn't seem to notice. "It was one of the things your father was interested in, too ..." He blushed. "Forgive me, I couldn't help but look through a few of the artefacts we dug out of the archives."

"It's fine," said Luke. "He'd be really happy to know people were still reading his research over a century and half later."

Dr Fontaine looked relieved. "Good. I can't say I understood it all, but he had some intriguing thoughts about the mechanism of the transformation. He was trying to find out exactly which property of moonlight causes the change. As you know, it doesn't have to be direct exposure. Coupled with modern findings in genetics, we've come up with a theory that it's actually an atmospheric condition – subatomic particles interacting with the werewolf gene."

Luke remembered the metal implants on the werewolves' heads.

"And could it be triggered artificially?"

"I suppose so," said Dr Fontaine. "But why would a

werewolf want to turn? It's generally seen as a curse, isn't it?"

"Maybe someone else put them there," said Luke. *And maybe we need to find out who.*

Aurora was looking the other way. "Enough talking," she said. "When are you going to try this stuff out?"

Twilight made the rolling moorland look like it was coated in a fine layer of ash. The rough bracken scraped Luke's thighs as he paced onward. The misty air was damp against his face. Around him, the dim torsos of the other Immortals were silhouetted against the clouds of blanket fog that rolled in, smothering the heath. Evelyn, of course, had vampiric night vision, and Aurora possessed something of the wolf's ability to see in dim light, even when in human form. So far, Luke had been relying on his own enhanced eyes, but he switched his ocular lens to infrared settings, and the figures around him took on shifting warm auras. The moors were cold and black. Nothing with a pulse was going to sneak up on him now.

Luke was hopeful the training exercise would be a success. Providing Harker made a swift recovery, they would be back in London in no time. He felt a twinge of worry, thinking of the city at the mercy of the werewolves, without the Immortals to protect it.

Shaking it off, Luke scanned the mist ahead. "OK, keep

your eyes peeled," he said. "Remember, this is a capture not kill exercise."

They were stalking along a muddy gully, about half a mile from the Foundation's HQ, and the ground sucked at Luke's boots. Raziel was gliding in circles at twenty feet, scanning the contours of the landscape. Luke realised he had no idea how a gargoyle's eyes worked – he'd have to run some tests when all this was over. If the giant stone creature didn't mind reading from an eye chart or having an ophthalmoscope shone directly into his retinas ...

Evelyn tripped over a half-hidden root, and Luke caught her before she fell.

"You all right?" he asked. Normally there was nothing clumsy about Evelyn.

She brushed him off, then shrugged, staring at the ground. "I guess I'm just thinking about Dad."

Luke nodded. Harker was still in the infirmary while Dr Fontaine's team ran tests on him, but if anything, he seemed to be getting worse, feverish and barely conscious. "You don't have to be out here," he said. "If you want to go back to him, no one will mind."

"He'd want me to focus," said Evelyn. "He's in the best hands. I just wish we'd brought him here sooner. I should have persuaded him."

"It's not your fault," said Luke.

"Incoming, four o'clock," rumbled Raziel from above.

Luke saw it too – two hundred yards and closing – the hunched glowing heat signature of a living body.

He lifted the net-gun, and Aurora unclipped a sonic grenade from her belt. The creature moved fast. Raziel folded his wings and dropped from the sky like a rock to block the creature's path. He thumped into the ground, swinging a wing to intercept, but the werewolf crouched and rolled beneath it. It kept coming.

"Now!" said Luke. Evelyn had disappeared from his side.

Aurora tossed the grenade. The creature flitted sideways, and Luke felt the impact in his eardrums as it hit the ground. The werewolf still hadn't slowed. It leapt through the air – a huge jump of ten or twelve metres. Luke lifted the barrel of the gun.

Ooomph!

Evelyn's staff caught the attacker mid-air, dropping it to the ground. She'd been hiding behind a tuft of long grass. Luke fired at the prone figure and the net closed over its squirming form. All of the Immortals gathered around as the thing cursed in colourful language.

Luke grinned. "Not bad," he said.

In the net, Dodger struggled in his heavy fur coat. He looked furious.

"I thought we was taking it gently," he said. "Blimmin' bat-girl here nearly took my head off."

"Sorry," said Evelyn. "We've got to make the exercise as real as possible." She rubbed her chin. "I think it could work," she said to the group. "With this weaponry and coordinated tactics it should be possible to capture a live werewolf. We just have to figure out a way of luring one out."

"Well, I was nearly a *dead* werewolf," said Dodger, as Luke untangled him.

"The bat thing is a myth, by the way," he said.

"He knows that," said Evelyn, smiling. "He just says it to annoy me."

"It'll take more than a tap with a staff to kill a lycanthrope," said Aurora.

Luke reloaded the net, and Evelyn folded her staff. Raziel stomped over to them.

"We need to ask Fontaine to increase the blast force of the sonic grenades if they're going to stun werewolves," Luke said. "That one barely slowed Dodger down, and the werewolves will be almost as quick."

Dodger grinned. "Yeah, if it hadn't been for Evelyn, I'd have got ya."

"Not likely," said Luke. "I had one more trick up my sleeve. Literally." He rolled up his sleeve and with just a thought, his lightning blade thrummed into life. "Fontaine's adapted it for werewolves," he said. "Vibrates with the same frequency as silver atoms – it should be just as effective as the metal itself in causing damage."

Aurora took a step back, looking troubled, so Luke slipped the blade away.

Her head jerked about and she sniffed the night air. "Werewolf," she said.

Dodger stood up, brushing down the coat. "I'm pretty sure this is *fake* fur," he said.

But Luke could tell from Aurora's body language that she was serious. She drew her Smith & Wesson and swung it round to point east. "It's near," she whispered.

Luke scanned the shadowy bracken, and swept his gaze along the crest of a barren hill, outlined against the navy sky. He strained his eyes. A few shrubs shuddered in the gentle breeze. "I see nothing," he said.

"My nose is better than your eyes," said Aurora, twitching her aim a fraction.

With his mouth dry, Luke switched back to infrared, and focused past her gun into the distance. *There.* A red blob, moving at a quick walk. His throat went dry. Then his peripheral vision picked up another, coming from the north. He spun around, counted five altogether, approaching their position from every direction. Most were on all fours, but one was standing. Their gait was pure werewolf.

Suddenly the training exercise had become very real. Where had they come from?

"They're surrounding us," he said. "Five of them. Defensive formation. Watch the flanks."

The Immortals went back to back, covering the angles. Evelyn quickly fastened silver spikes on to each end of her staff. Dodger checked his sleeves. Luke hoped he'd brought the silver fluoride as he let his lightning blade shimmer into life.

Footsteps came from each direction – the crunch of dry grass. Werewolves' heavy breathing. Luke's own breath came in rapid pants. Even though he tried to focus, he couldn't help the questions tumbling through his mind. *Were we followed? What do they want?* He cast a glance at Aurora, wondering again if it was something to do with her.

One of the shapes sped up, and Aurora swung the gun around. It went off with a crack and a muzzle flash, but the werewolf was already jumping. It slammed into her, paws-first. Aurora landed on her back, caught its snarling jaws in her hands, and with a twist, thrust the creature off. Luke dropped the net-gun and stabbed his lightning blade into the creature's side in a kendo thrust. The werewolf screeched in agony.

"Aurora – get back!" shouted Dodger. Luke saw his arm jerk and smoke exploded over them – scentless – but the other werewolves backed away. The silver fluoride worked, then. Evelyn drove at one with her staff, thrusting and spinning, but the creature caught it and raked at her with its other paw, tearing her trousers. She cried out and gripped her leg. Raziel clubbed the snarling attacker with a foot and sent it flying through the air. It was still trying to stand when he landed on its head, crushing its skull with a sickening crunch of bone. Raziel wiped his stone foot against the coarse heather, scraping off the bloodied fur.

Another werewolf ran at Luke, snout wrinkled over long incisors. Luke took a step back, holding the lightning blade up high, ready. Before it reached him, Dodger shot in front of it with a blur of speed and it toppled suddenly. Luke saw a thin tripwire wrapped around its ankles. He scrambled for the net-gun and fired the net, trapping the creature on the ground. It snapped and snarled, and Luke saw that the fibres began to cut into its flesh. It didn't even seem to notice, in its mindless struggle. Luke hit the electro-shock button and the furred thing stiffened and jerked, then lay still.

To his horror, the werewolf he had stabbed now rose to its feet. How was that possible? His lightning blade was supposed to be armed with silver. A blow like that should be near fatal.

"My lightning blade isn't working!" he shouted to the others. The creature shook its head groggily, and Luke saw its face shifting horribly, muzzle retracting back into a human lower jaw. The nose and eyes of the werewolf remained, wild and angry. It thrashed as its spine jerked straight, and its knee joints crunched into normal human legs, but its oversized paws remained armed with claws. *It's changing back*, thought Luke. Then it swung a long arm and he lifted his lightning blade to block the blow. Too late. Luke felt the impact as the paw smashed into his temple and dropped him to the ground. His head reeled as he tried to stand, but he saw Aurora leap forwards and deliver a punch to the werewolf's face. Its head jerked back.

"Tanner, stop!" she said. "It's me, Aurora, for Chrissakes."

For a split second, Luke thought he saw some human understanding in its eyes, then it roared through bloodied teeth and jumped at her. They tangled on the ground, and the sounds were like two rabid dogs tearing at one another. Luke saw it grab Aurora's hair and smash her head down hard. She looked dazed as it opened its mouth.

But instead of biting, it spoke.

"Coin!" it growled.

There was a loud bang, and Tanner's eyes widened. Then he toppled sideways. Aurora had her pistol in her hand, and the werewolf had a gaping wound in its stomach. After a brief shudder, it lay still.

Luke managed to roll on to his knees, sinking into the soggy peat. He tried to stand but fell back to the ground, still dizzy from the blow to the side of his head. Raziel, Dodger and Evelyn were all locked in combat. Everything was blurred and spinning, but he saw a shadow fall over him.

It was the werewolf trailing the remains of the net with it, bleeding from horrible wounds inflicted by the fibres.

It stared at him with hatred, then delivered a vicious kick to Luke's midriff. The air rushed from his lungs, which clenched like fists, squeezing the breath away while a deep paralysing pain seared through his chest.

CHAPTER 7

L uke crumpled into the heather. If it weren't for the metal alloy grafted to his bones, the kick would have easily broken his ribs. Luke fought for breath.

The bleeding werewolf threw off the net and fell on top of him, a terrible weight. With yellow eyes gleaming, it lifted its claws high to finish him off.

Luke raised his arm to protect himself and the claws sliced into his skin, breaking against the metal implants of his forearm. He jerked his hips in a judo throw and hurled the surprised werewolf sideways. He barely had time to marvel at his own reactions. His arm felt deadened and unresponsive, and he watched in horror as his attacker scrambled up into a crouch, ready to attack again.

Then the werewolf's eyes widened in shock. The next moment a silver spike erupted from its chest, dripping with blood. The werewolf's claws scrabbled at the tip, clutching it in disbelief, then it fell sideways, dead.

Evelyn stood over its corpse. She placed a foot on the creature's back, then yanked the staff out with one arm. Her other was clearly broken, the wrist hanging at a sickening angle. "You owe me," she said.

Luke winced at the pain from his ribs and arm. Raziel was still locked in combat. The gargoyle gripped a werewolf's wrists as they braced against one another. The werewolf was scraping and kicking with his legs, and snapping at Raziel's stone face. "Take him alive!" said Luke.

Raziel seemed to press harder, leaning right over the werewolf's body and bending it backwards. With a loud crunch, its spine snapped and it flopped to the ground.

There were only two werewolves left. Both were lumbering wildly after Dodger as he zipped around them with incredible speed. Their bodies were covered in gashes made by his jabbing silver dagger. He backed off, panting. "They won't give up," he gasped. "What am I supposed to do?"

Aurora took one out with a silver bullet to the head.

So much for taking them alive, Luke thought.

The other werewolf Dodger had been fighting dropped to its knees, a silver star lodged in its side. Its fur seemed to retract in a matter of seconds, and its body shrank to that of a smallish man. Luke recoiled. The man was a mess, face and body covered in wounds. He began to crawl towards

Aurora, pitifully slowly, reaching with trembling claws. She pointed her gun at him. "Stop there, Beecher!" she said.

Still he advanced, mindless but determined. Luke took a step forwards and planted a foot on his back. The man squirmed weakly.

"Careful, Luke," said Raziel.

"He's got an implant," said Luke, pointing at the metal lozenge on the man's neck. It was only about two inches long, and an inch wide.

"Pull it out," said Aurora.

Luke looked around. No more attackers were coming. He reached down and gripped the implant. He hesitated for a second, steadying his hand. Then he focused his strength and pulled it out carefully. The man groaned as it came loose, leaving bloody gouges in the flesh of his neck either side of his spine. The implant had long spikes on the rear side, which had obviously been embedded deep into the werewolf's brainstem.

The man on the ground rolled over, eyes distant, his blood-covered lips parted slightly. Luke felt a swell of sympathy. Aurora crouched at his side, while Evelyn and Dodger came closer.

"Is there anything we can do?" asked Luke.

Aurora grimaced. "I doubt it."

Then, through the blood, the man smiled. "Thank you," he said.

Luke glanced up at Evelyn, whose frown must have mirrored his own. *Thank you?* For what?

The light left the werewolf's eyes and his head rolled to one side. Aurora felt for a pulse on his blood-slicked neck and shook her head.

Luke surveyed the carnage of dead creatures. They'd attacked relentlessly, without thought for their own survival.

"They didn't care if they died," said Evelyn. She was breathing hard. "Did you see that one in the net – it almost killed *itself* struggling to get to Luke."

Luke held out the piece of metal on his palm. "Or they didn't have a choice," he said. "These things must be controlling them – sending electrical signals through the spinal cord into the brain."

"Bit of a hunch, innit?" said Dodger.

"I think he's right," said Aurora. "Why else would Beecher thank us for taking him out?"

"Beecher?" said Evelyn.

Aurora nodded to the bloodied man. "I knew him," she said. "A long time ago."

Luke looked at her. "The other one asked you for a coin," he said. "You know what's going on, don't you?"

Aurora straightened. "I have an idea," she replied. She reached into her pocket and took out her silver dime.

"That?" said Dodger. "I ain't havin' a laugh, but these chaps didn't come looking to mug you."

"There's something I haven't told you about the coin," Aurora said, tossing and catching it. "In truth, I often forget about it myself."

"Go on," said Evelyn. She cradled her wrist, and Luke heard a crunch as the bones knitted back together.

Aurora looked at the dead werewolves. "Let's get back to the base," she said. "They need to clear up these bodies before morning. I'll fill you all in there."

"They called him the Soul Hunter," said Aurora, as she disassembled her Smith & Wesson on the table.

They were back in the underground weapons lab, waiting for Dr Fontaine. It was near to dawn outside, but without any windows, it could have been any time. Certainly no one was thinking about sleep, apart from Dodger, rocking back on the back legs of his chair, his yawns getting more theatrical by the moment.

Luke lay on a table, pads taped to his torso while BIOS ran diagnostics on his body. Evelyn had injected healing accelerants into his gashes and cuts, and they were already well scabbed-over. In the brushed steel of a cabinet, he saw a blurred reflection of his face. The bruise where he'd been whacked by the werewolf had faded to a yellow-green.

A recon team organised by Dr Fontaine had headed out on to Dartmoor to scrape up what remained of the werewolves for testing. Luke guessed the secrets, if there were any, would be found inside the metal implant. He wished they could make use of Harker's keen mind, but Evelyn's dad was only getting worse. For now at least, the Immortals were going to have to face whatever they were up against without their leader.

"So why didn't you kill this 'Soul Hunter' when you 'ad the chance?" asked Dodger.

"Weren't you listening?" said Evelyn. "He's immortal."

"Yeah, but so am I," said Dodger. "Don't mean I'll survive if you cut my 'ead off."

"Draka is very powerful," said Aurora. "He's a spirit. Like other Soul Hunters before him, he inhabits a vessel called the Blood Armour. It's a magical body that can regenerate in seconds, even from decapitation. Draka absorbs the spirits of those he kills, and we think he can control the minds of other creatures. Predators, especially."

"So this geezer's impossible to kill?" said Dodger. "Marvellous."

Aurora sighed. "We ripped the spirit of Draka from the Blood Armour and imprisoned him. But the Blood Armour retained its regenerative power, even without Draka inside it. Indestructible."

"And the Blood Armour's in Louisiana?" said Luke.

"Protected by magic," said Aurora.

"And Draka himself?" asked Evelyn.

Aurora placed her hand palm down on the table. "He's in here," she said.

Luke jumped off the table, wincing, and stared at Aurora's hand. "Where?"

She lifted it to reveal her silver dime.

"Draka is in your coin?" he said.

Aurora nodded a fraction.

They all peered closer. "You sure?" said Dodger.

"As sure as I can be," said Aurora. "These werewolves – they've come from Louisiana. If whoever is controlling them wants the coin ... there's only one reason why."

"To release Draka," muttered Raziel. He was standing guard by the door.

"Well, let's melt the thing down," said Dodger. "Destroy it."

Aurora shook her head. "If we did that, Draka would be released."

"Hide it then," said Evelyn. "Bury it in concrete or stick it in a fruit machine."

"No," said Aurora. "The werewolves might track it down. They've managed so far."

Luke stared at the silver disc. He thought he knew everything about the Immortals – everything important, anyway. And "important" definitely included carrying round an ancient demon with you for centuries.

"Did Dad know about this?" said Evelyn, staring at Aurora.

Aurora wiped down the gun barrel. "I've told no one. The fewer people who know about it, the better."

Evelyn shook her head in frustration. "You should have trusted us! We're supposed to be a team."

Aurora snapped back the barrel and slammed the magnum on to the table. "It's my burden to bear! My responsibility." Her shoulders sagged as she sighed deeply, then she looked up, a far-off expression on her face. "It's personal."

"We need to find out who's behind the mind tech," said Luke.

"Agreed," said Aurora. "I've seen enough of my old pack killed."

"So what's the plan?" said Dodger. "Analyse the implant, look for clues there?"

Aurora stood up and slipped her pistol into its harness. "I'm going to Louisiana."

"Er . . . come again?" said Dodger.

"That's where the werewolves came from," she said, "and that's where the Blood Armour is imprisoned. I'm going to find some answers."

Luke jumped up from the table, grabbing his satchel from the floor. He wasn't sure about leaving without Harker, but it sounded like they didn't have a choice. "OK, we can take the Foundation's private plane. Let's gather up—"

"No," said Aurora. "I'm going alone."

Luke stopped dead in his tracks, staring at Aurora, the words unable to sink in. Evelyn was shaking her head slowly, her pale cheeks reddening in fury. Even Dodger was speechless, balancing on the back legs of his chair and gawping at Aurora.

"You can't leave us," Evelyn whispered.

"She's right!" Luke said, finding his voice. "We should stick together."

Aurora donned her hat. "That wouldn't work. I need to earn the werewolves' trust. No offence, but dragging a couple of kids along for the ride won't help."

"I'm not just some kid," Luke said, voice raised. A well of emotion he'd been bottling up since they arrived at the Foundation was suddenly crashing through him. "My dad was Victor Frankenstein. In case you don't remember, I killed Sanakhte, while you were locked up in a silver cage!" Luke blinked, shocked at his own outburst. "Sorry," he said. Now it had been released, the anger was draining away. "What I'm trying to say is, Evelyn's right. We are a team – that's how the Immortals work, that's how we're strongest."

Aurora packed her gun in her belt. "I see what you're saying, and I know you can handle yourself. But to the pack, you're just an outsider. Look, stay here. Help Harker get better. Work with Fontaine. I'll keep a low profile, just in case we're being watched. If all goes well, I should be back in a couple of days."

"And if it doesn't go well?" asked Evelyn.

Aurora cocked her head in a shrug. "Assume the worst."

Luke didn't like her tone at all. It was clear she was putting a brave face on. Truth was, she sounded out of her depth, just like the rest of them.

"I don't think we should split up," he said firmly. "You signed the Founding Document. You pledged yourself to the Immortals."

Aurora stared hard at him. "And I'm keeping my oath. I'll just be apart from the rest of you for a while."

Luke could see she wasn't going to budge. Her mind was made up. And Luke didn't like it one bit. *We've lost Harker, and now Aurora.* Luke tried to keep faith, to believe it was only temporary. But the creeping anxiety only grew. Doubts that had been gathering in his mind formed themselves into one terrible thought: *The Immortals are breaking apart.*

And Luke was powerless to stop it.

It was still dark outside when Aurora's taxi rolled up the long driveway. Luke's arm was in a sling, and his body felt bruised, but the pain was nothing compared to the deep feeling of unease crawling in his gut.

The black sedan parked up, and the driver clambered out, opening the boot. His bleary eyes widened when he saw Aurora approach.

"Exeter airport," she said, throwing her case into the boot. "And make it fast."

"Sure," the man mumbled, hurrying back to the driver's seat.

Luke could almost feel Evelyn's anger as she stood beside him in the doorway of the Foundation. Dodger was more concerned about another ambush, eyes darting round the grounds. Even though there were hundreds of high-tech cameras on the fences, Raziel had offered to take to the skies again in order to patrol the perimeter of the estate. Luke felt reassured to have him out there. But it was clearly not offering much comfort to Dodger.

Aurora strode up to them. "Well, I guess I'll see you around. I'll let you know if I find anything. You keep yourselves safe. Send my best wishes to Harker."

Evelyn nodded curtly. "Bye."

"Yeah, good luck and all that," said Dodger, rubbing his tired eyes. "But seriously, don't get eaten or anything."

Aurora grunted, then turned to Luke. Despite his doubts, Luke put on a brave face. "Good luck," he said.

"Thanks," she said. "There's something else." She reached out a fist, opening it to reveal the silver dime in her palm. "Hold on to this for me," she said. "We need to keep it as far from Draka's body as possible."

Luke was speechless. "Me?"

Evelyn frowned. "Maybe Raziel should hold on to it. Or I don't mind taking it."

"Luke can manage," said Aurora. "You heard him. He was the one who defeated Sanakhte, while I was in a silver cage." She grinned. "But you lot make sure you back him up."

Luke hesitated then held out his hand. "OK ... If you think it's best." Aurora pressed the dime into his palm and he looked down at it, stunned.

"Right," said Aurora. "That's everything." She turned around.

Luke caught her arm. "Are you sure about this?" he asked.

"I'm sure," she said. She slapped Luke on the shoulder. "You'll be fine." Then she turned and paced to the cab. She crammed her huge frame into the back seat, and the cab moved off. Luke watched it go up the drive, then exit through the gates in the distance.

"That's that," said Evelyn.

"Well, I for one am gonna get some kip," said Dodger. "Wake me up if anything interesting happens."

Luke closed his fingers around the coin. It felt just like any other. But according to Aurora, it could be one of the most dangerous objects in the world. Their enemy, whoever was controlling the werewolves, had first come to London looking for it, then somehow tracked them to Dartmoor.

He should have felt safe, surrounded by the other Immortals, in a high security facility. But now they were only four, with no leader and no plan. *We're more vulnerable than ever.*

As Luke slipped the coin into his inside jacket pocket, he felt like a target.

CHAPTER 8

L uke was sitting at the table in the underground weapons lab, turning the coin over in his fingers. In the hours since Aurora had given it to him, he hadn't felt any kind of dark influence. Nothing like the bouts of rage and violence that the heart of Sanakhte had brought on in Luke – though the heart had been *inside* him.

He looked over to where Evelyn was combat training, spinning and thrusting her staff with precise stabs and vicious swipes. She clearly needed to release some steam. Dodger was slumped in a chair opposite Luke, snoring loudly. Luke sighed, frustration building. They shouldn't just be waiting down here. Dr Fontaine was preparing the bodies of the werewolves for autopsy, and suggested they stay out of the way – Dr Pavlovic was bound to be sensitive about the attack. Luke guessed that was probably an understatement.

He sat up and pored over his scrapbook lying on the table for what must be the tenth time. He'd written everything down but still had so many questions ... How had the werewolves managed to track them to Southwark and then to the Foundation? Who had sent them? What did they want with Draka?

Evelyn came over, panting. "That guy can sleep anywhere," she said, frowning at Dodger.

"Comes from all those decades squatting in abandoned buildings and living on the street," said Luke. In his spare time, he'd been interviewing Dodger about his life over the last century and a half. The pickpocket had been far from forthcoming, fidgeting non-stop through their meetings. Depending on his mood, Dodger either claimed to have forgotten events or elaborated so much that Luke had no idea what was truth and what was Dodger's pure imagination. Hard evidence had proved a more reliable source. It was like being a historian, trawling through old newspapers and archives looking for clues.

"I'm sick of this waiting," said Evelyn. "Fontaine must be ready for us now."

"Yeah," said Luke. He got to his feet, dropping the coin in his pocket. "Come on, I can't wait around any longer."

"What about Pavlovic?" said Evelyn. "She won't like us being around."

"She'll just have to deal with it," said Luke.

They took the elevator up to the main corridors of the Foundation. Luke touched the coin in his pocket and tried to feel confident. Aurora had entrusted it to him. He wouldn't let her down.

"She should have told us before," said Evelyn, as they passed scientists eyeing them curiously. It took Luke a moment to realise she was thinking about Aurora too. "I mean, if she had that coin the whole time, it was putting us all in danger."

"I guess she never expected it to come to this," said Luke.

"I don't know why you're defending her," said Evelyn. "She's always liked to do things on her own, outside the team."

"Because my father trusted her," Luke said simply.

The door at the far end of the corridor opened and Dr Pavlovic strode towards them. Luke froze. Her face was deadly serious.

"I've been looking for you," she said. "I've ordered maximum security protocols."

"Best to take precautions," said Evelyn archly.

Dr Pavlovic pursed her lips. "I knew it was a bad idea you just showing up like this. But I didn't think you would lure a gang of werewolves to the moors for a fight!"

Luke didn't know what to say, but Evelyn cut in.

"Sorry for the inconvenience," she said. "Don't let us nearly getting ripped apart ruin your beauty sleep."

Dr Pavlovic's eyes flashed dangerously. For a moment Luke saw how formidable she could be. "Miss Harker, there are around one hundred and fifty scientists resident at the Foundation. They are all the leading proponents in their chosen fields. *Scientists*. Not soldiers. Not fighters. I am responsible for their well-being. Now, I respect your father a great deal, but you must understand I cannot allow your presence to endanger their lives."

"We understand," said Luke, putting his hand on Evelyn's arm. She looked about ready to explode. "Raziel is out there now, keeping watch."

Dr Pavlovic snorted. "Oh good. I'll rest easy knowing there's a gargoyle flying over my head." The doctor kept on past them without a backwards glance.

"I don't often get the temptation to bite a human," muttered Evelyn, when Dr Pavlovic was out of earshot, "but for her I could make an exception."

Luke grinned. He was just glad that Evelyn's mind seemed to be off her dad for a bit. "Come on, let's find Fontaine."

He was in the infirmary, in what used to be the house's drawing room on the ground floor. Not that any of the old rugs or furniture remained. Luke vaguely remembered his mother's piano had rested against one wall, and a huge gilt-edged mirror had once dominated the wall above the fireplace. Now there were several tracks holding curtains running along the strip-lighted ceiling, a polished concrete floor, and lots of medical equipment, plus a bank of computers and several office chairs. The windows had been blocked up, presumably to ensure privacy and a sterile environment. Fontaine was leaning over a 3D monitor as they arrived. The holographic image of a body floated in mid-air. There was a curtain drawn behind him.

"Luke! Miss Harker!" he said. "How are you?"

"We're fine," said Evelyn. "Have you got anything on the implant?"

"I was going to brief you shortly," said Dr Fontaine. "Will the others be joining us?"

"Raziel's on patrol," said Luke. "Dodger's ... erm ... "

"Strategic planning," put in Evelyn.

"And Aurora Cage?" asked Dr Fontaine.

"She's just gone for some air," Luke lied, thinking he should keep the Immortals' actions as secret as possible – he didn't want anything getting back to Dr Pavlovic. "She sort of does her own thing a lot of the time."

"A lone wolf." Dr Fontaine smiled. "Speaking of which ... "

He stood up and whipped back the curtain. Luke gasped. On the top of a wheeled stretcher lay one of the dead werewolves, the one called Tanner, still in human form. His naked body was covered in a sheet, but from his grizzled face and grey hair, Luke guessed he had been about sixty when he was turned. He realised the image on the monitor was of the corpse in front of him.

"I've examined the physiology of the specimen," said Dr Fontaine. "There's nothing untoward, besides the strands of lupine DNA."

"What about the implant?" said Luke. "He had one in his neck, didn't he?"

"I haven't got round to that yet," said Dr Fontaine.

Evelyn went to the 3D display and began to manipulate the image with her hands, zooming and rotating for a better look. She isolated the brain, and peered closer.

"Looks like the implant embedded right into the basal ganglia," she said.

"And that means mind control, right?" said Luke.

"I would hesitate to use that exact term," said Dr Fontaine, "but potentially the manipulation of neural functions on a number of levels – movement, emotion, cognition."

"Sounds like mind control to me," said Evelyn. "You didn't see them, Doctor. They had no thought for their own well-being. They were like kamikaze pilots."

Dr Fontaine raised his eyebrows. "Fascinating. I've never seen anything like it."

Luke stared at the complex brain wiring with a mixture of awe and fear. Whoever was behind it was a formidable enemy. And now Luke had the coin, they were coming after him. "Who'd have the knowledge to do something like this?" asked Luke.

"Maybe three or four scientists in the world," said Dr Fontaine. "I've communicated with most of them over the years."

"Can you make a list?" asked Luke.

"Yes, I can," said Dr Fontaine, "but it makes little sense to me. The question is why they'd do such a thing?"

Luke was about to ask Dr Fontaine why his lightning blade hadn't been a hundred per cent effective against the werewolf when another question wormed into his head.

"Could an implant make a werewolf turn, even when it's not a full moon?"

Dr Fontaine pushed out his lip as he pondered. "That's really not my area of . . . Hang on." A light at his belt flashed in time with a low-level buzzing. Dr Fontaine looked briefly at Evelyn. "Oh, no . . . Jonathan."

"What's the matter?" said Evelyn, face draining of blood.

Dr Fontaine's white coat flapped behind him as he ran from the room. Luke and Evelyn sped after him. "Wait! What's happening?" pleaded Evelyn.

They raced out of the house and sprinted across the gravel to the separate unit where Harker was being treated. Evelyn was quicker than both Luke and Dr Fontaine, but the double doors were coded. "Let us in!" she said, banging hard.

Luke saw Raziel above, angling down in a dive.

Dr Fontaine got there too, breathing heavily, and tapped in the access code. They burst through the doors and straight away Luke heard a pained growling. A heart monitor was beeping rapidly and a computerised voice was repeating over and over: "Cardiac arrest imminent."

"Report," barked Dr Fontaine, going at once to a monitor and tapping several places to read through displays.

"He's having a fit," said a woman in blue doctor's scrubs. She was holding one of Harker's arms, while another doctor lay across his legs. Harker thrashed, and foamed from his lips. His entire body was soaked with sweat.

"Dad!" cried Evelyn, rushing forward.

"We need to stabilise," said Dr Fontaine. "Miss Harker, stay back, please." He twisted from the monitor and picked up a syringe. "Hold him steady," he said.

But before he was even close, Harker lurched, lifting the female doctor off her feet and hurling her across the room with incredible force. She slammed into a tray table, scattering instruments. Luke rushed to her side.

The other doctor had no chance. As soon as one of Harker's flailing legs came free, he kicked the doctor in the chest, dropping him instantly. Dr Fontaine hung back, suddenly afraid, as Harker continued to thrash and jerk randomly. "Restrain him!" said Luke, as he dragged the female doctor to a safe corner.

Raziel came to the rescue. Harker was superhumanly strong, but he was no match for solid stone. The gargoyle pinned him with an arm across the chest, and a wing across his knees, as Harker's fists became bloody from pounding his unyielding grey chest. Then he suddenly lay still, as if some evil spirit had left his body.

"Help me with the straps," said Dr Fontaine, and Luke left the doctor propped against the wall, stepping in to fasten down Harker's wrists and ankles. Evelyn, behind him, seemed completely shell-shocked. As the room calmed, and the two doctors huddled together, Luke became aware of the soft beep of the heart monitor once more.

"What happened?" asked Evelyn.

Dr Fontaine, looking shaken himself, moved to a computer terminal, and tapped a few times on the screen. Charts flashed up. "Looks like a sudden accumulation of red blood cells, and some sort of hormone I don't recognise. It's flooded his hippocampus." He ran a hand over his skull. "I really don't know what we're dealing with here."

"BDS," said Raziel.

Evelyn, fighting back tears, came forward slowly and touched her father's cheek. "Don't let him die," she said. "Please."

Dodger arrived at last. "Heard the commotion," he

said. "What's up?" He saw Harker, the shaken doctors and scattered and broken equipment. "Dearie me."

Dr Fontaine took a deep breath. "We'll do everything we can," he said, "but without access to more research, I'll admit we're acting blind."

Luke looked at some of the readouts on the monitors. Harker's core temperature was seventy-five degrees, way too high for a vampire. From the warning signals on the full-body diagnostic, it looked like his liver and kidneys were close to shutting down. Evelyn was looking too, her eyes wet.

For the first time, it really hit Luke. *He's not getting better at all. He's dying, slowly, in front of us.*

Harker had always been like an uncle to him – kinder than he needed to be. And it had been Harker who worked tirelessly for over a century to fulfil Victor's final wish and bring Luke back from the dead. He literally owed his life to Evelyn's father.

He backed away from the monitor and put his arm around his friend, feeling utterly helpless. He knew what it was like to be without a dad, though he'd been lucky not to see his own die. Luke felt completely powerless. If a scientist like Dr Fontaine couldn't work out what to do . . .

But perhaps there was another option.

"I've got an idea," he said.

Evelyn and Dr Fontaine looked at him.

"My dad's papers," Luke said. "He studied vampires for years before he even met Evelyn's father. He collected manuscripts and pamphlets and research from all over the world. If there's an answer to the Blood Deprivation Syndrome, it might be here, in his old study."

Evelyn wiped her eyes, and Luke saw a spark of hope gleaming in them. "You could be right."

Dr Fontaine nodded slowly. "It's as good a chance as any," he said.

But Luke noticed he didn't look them in the eye. "How long do you think we have?" he asked Fontaine.

The doctor rubbed the back of his head, and glanced at Evelyn nervously. "From the rate of organ failure, I would say . . . a day. Maybe a day and a half, at best."

They raced to the study, barging through groups of disgruntled scientists. Raziel and Dodger stayed with Dr Fontaine to provide protection for the doctors, in case Harker had any more violent episodes.

Soon, Luke and Evelyn reached the original part of the manor, charging their way through the tiled corridors until they reached Luke's father's old study. Luke pushed open the mahogany doors and was met with the smell of leather and wax. The scents of learning. Luke felt a deep pang in his heart. *I won't let Evelyn lose her dad like I lost mine.*

"Where do we start?" said Evelyn, voice frantic.

Luke lit a lamp on the table, casting the room in a warm glow. He paced the room, glancing at the shelves of books. Somewhere among them lay a clue to saving Harker's life – at least that's what he hoped.

"They're not in much of an order," he said.

But there were large sections of his father's library that he discounted straight away. Travelogues from across the ages. Newtonian physics. Witchcraft and demonology. Mathematics and geometry. Alchemical writings. Shamanic texts. Luke was awed by the breadth of his father's reading. There had to be something about vampire illnesses somewhere.

Luke directed Evelyn to start searching a section of shelves with some potentially vampire-related texts. He went to a chest, and found it stuffed with scrolls. His father's dog-eared notebooks were stacked in a drawer. Just seeing his father's almost illegible scrawl forced him to swallow back his grief. He remembered seeing Victor Frankenstein leaning over his desk late into the night, lit only by candle, dipping his quill and scratching away at the page, or gazing vacantly as his mind struggled with a problem. What he would do for his father's keen mind now.

As Luke scanned the notebooks it was clear they covered a vast array of topics, seemingly in no order at all. Some were straightforward journals, but in others the text was packed tight around equations or diagrams. If a cure to the vampire disease lay in them, it might take days to find. *Days won't help Harker.*

Luke's eyes repeatedly flicked to the old grandfather clock standing opposite the desk. The hours seemed to gallop past as they whittled the material down into a promising pile, and began to inspect in more detail. Victor Frankenstein had been interested in vampires from a young age, it seemed. He had travelled in Europe and South America following even the smallest clues. Vampires existed in the legends and myths of many cultures, suggesting to Luke the different lines had evolved in isolation from one another, a genetic mutation from the humans upon which they preyed.

There were notes from a dig in North Africa – on the Tunisian border – where Victor had unearthed a vampire tomb and exhumed the body to carry out an autopsy. Evelyn winced as they looked at the detailed anatomical drawings and descriptions. But nothing there was useful to them.

Luke carried on scouring the books, trying to make sure he didn't miss anything. Time seemed to slip by faster than ever. He looked at the clock. Five hours had already passed. Luke put aside a seventeenth-century pamphlet purporting to be about a travelling vampire circus, when he realised Evelyn hadn't spoken for some time. Looking up, he saw she was sat on the floor, reading a handwritten piece of paper, weeping silently.

"What is it?" he said.

Evelyn sniffed, wiped her cheek, and gestured to a bundle of similar papers. "Letters," she said. "From my father to yours."

Luke edged closer and peered over her shoulder. The letter Evelyn was reading was dated August 1852. He scanned the text.

My dear Victor,

You know well the esteemed trust in which I hold you, and I pray I do not flatter myself to think the sentiments reciprocated. Your friendship is one of the constants in my life's firmament, a source of solace and deep contentment. The second, you are well aware, is my precious Evelyn.

Though I can never forgive myself for the curse I have brought upon her – turned by that fiend Dracula's slaves into a creature of the night – I can only strive to make her immortal life as fulfilling as possible. Though she is still, to the uninformed eye, a thirteen-year-old girl, she has already lived for a quarter-century. She is a girl no longer, and it is selfish of me to pretend she can find purpose in only girlish pursuits. It is for that reason I entreat you, my friend, to allow her to join us in our clandestine group. She is strong, resourceful, quick-witted. Above all, she has the courage of a lion.

I can imagine how you will baulk on reading this, but please consider carefully. I have thought long and hard on

the topic and I believe with all my heart that Evelyn can be
an Immortal in deed as well as fact.

   Ever yours,

   JH

Evelyn's tear splashed on the page, and Luke eased it from her hand, setting it on top of the others to one side.

"I can't live without him," she said. She looked tired and defeated, turning her gaze to the room. "But there's nothing here that can help."

"We'll find a cure," Luke replied softly. "I promise. Let's keep looking."

He passed her more books and journals, while he went back to the shelves. Luke focused on the later works of his father and, after just another couple of minutes, his heart leapt as he came across a small illuminated book with ancient script on the front. His translation upload kicked in automatically. He knew several languages – even Cockney rhyming slang – but he identified this as a variation of a Coptic script.

It read: *The Physiology of Vampires.*

"I think I might have found something," he said, opening the delicate, mottled pages. Evelyn climbed to her feet, dropping a book before hurrying over.

Luke slowly flicked through, until something caught his eye. Under a section on "Disease", he translated, "Blood denial and its effects, by Brother Pietr Domicus."

"Go on," said Evelyn, her voice a little hoarse.

Luke read aloud, stiltedly, as his brain converted the writing to English.

"To the subject of blood denial and its effects, the most extreme forms can cause debilitating and irreversible thirst. In such cases, no volume of consumption can quench the great drought within, just as no rainfall can flood the desert sands. In time, the subject will suffer loss of mental faculties, retreating to the primal state of animalistic rage, violence, and eventually the loss of all human character."

Luke paused.

"Go on," said Evelyn quietly.

"With no cure possible, a vampire suffering thus may choose to end his or her time on the Earth by their own hand, or one close may take pity and commit the final act on their behalf."

He stopped again, wishing he could take back the words.

Evelyn turned and walked towards the window silently. Luke didn't know what to say as her shoulders shook. He looked hopelessly at the foreign words.

"Evelyn ..."

"There's no cure," she said. "That's what it means."

Luke turned the page, eyes searching for a shred of hope, but the text moved on to other matters. He sighed and lowered his head. "That was written hundreds of years ago," he said. "Just because the author didn't know a way to heal it, doesn't mean we can't find one. With Fontaine's help ..."

"Don't, Luke," said Evelyn. "I know you mean well, but don't. It's over."

CHAPTER 9

Louisiana

Aurora stepped out of the revolving door of the arrivals terminal at Louis Armstrong New Orleans Airport and tried to get her bearings. She knew from a map on the plane's entertainment system that the airport was south of Lake Pontchartrain, and north of the Mississippi River. The predawn air was still humid. She closed her eyes and drew in a deep breath through her nostrils. She could just make out the scent of the river – the fragrance of the water, and the earthy odour of the sediment it carried. But it was faint, buried beneath the harsh smells of the city: car fumes, tarmac, concrete, fried food, the sweat of the taxi drivers waiting at the ranks in front of her. And there was another scent she recognised . . .

"Hello, Cole," she said. She turned. He was leaning against a wall, watching her.

"Changed, hasn't it?" he said.

"Just a bit."

After over one hundred and seventy years, he looked just the same as she remembered. Stubbled jaw, long black hair and high cheekbones. Lumberjack shirt, ripped jeans, leather boots and jacket, despite the fact it was pushing eighty degrees even at night. He cracked a grin.

"No luggage, Cage?"

"Travelling light," she replied, walking over. Actually, she'd had to leave her case in London. She didn't realise you had to check it in before going through security. It had taken every ounce of patience not to retaliate when the security officers took it off her and insisted on carrying out a full body search. She stopped in front of Cole. For a second she didn't know what to do.

Cole held up a hand and she gripped it in a firm shake.

"Been a while," she said.

"Too long."

He was squeezing, but she squeezed harder until he started to look uncomfortable.

"Same old Cage," he said, pulling free.

Aurora scanned the lanes in front of the terminal. Regular folk lugging cases. Farewells and greetings. The harsh lights of the cars and buses. They were different to

London. The cabs were yellow or white and the buses were more like coaches. It seemed strange. Alien. "Where's the rest of the pack?" she asked.

Cole shrugged. "You didn't give us a whole lotta time," he said. "Things have changed, Cage. You shouldn't have left that message . . ."

"How else was I going to get in touch? Lucky for me you're still going to the same bar after a hundred and eighty years."

"It's our clubhouse now. You were lucky the message got to me. Some of the others . . . Let's just say the pack might not be happy with a new wolf in town."

"They better get used to it," Aurora replied.

Cole grinned at her. "Same old Cage." He paused and the smile faded. "Is it true Beecher and Tanner are dead?"

Aurora nodded.

Cole's jawline tightened. "They were good guys. Knew them for nearly two centuries. And Draka—"

"Not here," said Aurora. "We taking a taxi?"

Cole cocked his head. "Hell, no. Follow me."

He led her to a parking lot attached to the terminal, up a set of stairs to the third level. They strode past rows of vehicles. Aurora glanced out at a criss-cross of densely packed buildings sprawling to the east. Last time she'd been here all this was swampland. She'd been out this way more than once on a full moon, preying on deer. *Better them than people*. Back then, it had been ten miles before you met any settlement – clusters of cottages and town houses and the grand French colonial buildings that hadn't burned down in the great fire. Then, further south, the heaving port built on the banks of the river. When she'd left for London she'd made a point of not looking back, and now she wondered if any of it still existed.

She rolled her shoulders, clicking the muscles in her back. Plane seats weren't designed for people nearly two metres tall and over a hundred kilos.

"Good flight?" said Cole.

"Slower than an Alaskan winter," Aurora said. She'd taken off and landed in the dark but hadn't slept at all during the entire nine hours. She'd been wedged between a suit who seemed to be drinking himself to an early grave and a sixty-year-old Texan divorcee who wouldn't shut up about her fourth husband's gambling problem. Hadn't even taken the hint when Aurora tipped her hat over her eyes and pretended to snooze. She wondered how Luke and the others were getting on. Reached for the coin, then remembered it wasn't there.

She told herself she'd done the right thing. Keeping distance between the coin and the Blood Armour was the safest option. Plus, those werewolves would be coming after her – she'd made no secret of leaving the Foundation and booking the flight. Whoever had been following her would know where to find her now. The thought caused a prickle to pass down her back, and she couldn't help glancing over her shoulder.

Cole stopped by two black and chrome motorcycles. The logo on the chassis was a black and silver eagle – Harley-Davidsons. Cole fished in his pocket, nodded to the bike on the left with the slung-back saddle and twin exhaust, and tossed Aurora a set of keys. "Yours is the SuperLow. You can ride, right?"

Aurora tried to smile. "Sure," she said.

She swung her leg over the cushioned saddle and looked for somewhere to insert the key. Found it on the fuselage. Luckily Cole wasn't paying attention as he zipped up his jacket. The last thing she'd ridden on American soil was a horse. When she'd boarded the ship to England, automobiles hadn't even been invented.

She turned the key and the bike grumbled into life beneath her.

"Where to?" asked Cole.

"The clubhouse," said Aurora.

Cole frowned. "I'm not sure that's such a great idea, Cage. They might not be ... friendly."

"Just take me to them," said Aurora. "Trust me, it's important."

"Fine," said Cole. "They're in the city. Keep up if you can."

He twisted the throttle and surged forwards across the car lot. Aurora kicked away her stand and did the same. The bike lurched off with a squeal of brakes, then shuddered to a halt. *This might take some getting used to.*

Aurora's gaze flickered between the two levers attached to each of the wide handlebars. *Clutch. Brake. Clutch. Brake.* It seemed simple enough, if you didn't have to think about everything else you were doing too. She pulled back the clutch and flicked the gear lever. Then she twisted the throttle. Too early. The bike's monstrous engine roared in protest. But then it clicked into top gear and the bike kicked forward. She sped up alongside Cole. Actually, riding a bike was a hell of a lot of fun.

They were cruising along the freeway. The ground was dead flat, and changed completely from the last time she was here. It had all been fields then, lined with the threads of irrigation channels. Now it was all concrete. Trees had become street lights and traffic signals. Riverbanks tamed by flood defences. People drove around in pickups, trucks and sedans, going about their business, where once you could have walked for days and not seen another breathing soul. Bars with elaborate fluorescent signage – Madame Arrete's, Lulu's, Pierre's Place – glowed dully among the sprawling malls and businesses. She saw a family trying to shepherd their two kids into a restaurant, as the kids yelled at each other. Aurora felt a jolt in her chest. *About the same ages as Europa and Lysidas.*

Her thoughts turned dark.

All this is at risk. If Draka returns, he'll spare nothing.

A modern city like this would offer the Soul Hunter an almost infinite feast. It would be a massacre, the death toll racking up as Draka fed off their spirits. No one would be able to stop him. And where would he go next? Lafayette? New York? London?

After a couple of miles, Cole steered off towards the bay. They passed between large wooden houses that looked abandoned, looming at the roadside, then out across raised roadways. There were few other vehicles out on the road here, and she opened the bike's throttle until the speedometer hit seventy. The Harley could probably give twice that.

Cole pulled level, then ahead, signalling right.

On to a single track. A small building in the distance.

Bikes parked up alongside a glorified shack with a flickering sign that simply read "Beer & Liqu r". Muted sounds of heavy metal music. Cole parked up, and Aurora eased her ride to a halt beside him.

"This is where they spend their days," he said.

Aurora sensed his caution. If a tough-guy like Cole was nervous, so was she.

"Let me go in first," said Cole.

"I don't think so," said Aurora.

"Cage, they—"

But she was already heading up the creaking steps to the screen door. She pushed it open and took a step inside.

Smoke-filled air. Pool table to the right, three people standing beside it – two men and a woman. Bar straight ahead – two stools out of five occupied. Jukebox pumping out music right beside her. Barmaid pouring shots. She spilled some tequila across the bar top when she saw Aurora.

Everyone turned. Dull stares, apart from one huge guy sitting off to the left, on his own with his back to her. There was something about his silhouette ... A jacket hung over the back of his chair with the picture of a wolf's profile across the back, and the words "Wolf Pack" emblazoned above.

"How original," said Aurora.

That caused one of the barflies to scrape back his chair. No, *her* chair. Aurora searched her memory as the woman gazed coldly at her, knowing the face was in there somewhere.

Red Fur's girlfriend. Tina? Trish? She must have been turned at some point, because Aurora remembered her being a normal human. The pouty blonde face had hardened in a century and a half. *Maybe Red Fur did it, before he died.*

"Hey," said Aurora.

Tina or Trish turned back to her drink. The others

focused on their pool game. The guy facing away moved a fraction. His massive fist curled on the table in front of him. Aurora could smell the danger in the room, laced with cigarette smoke, sweat and stale booze.

Cole had come in behind Aurora. He took her elbow and gave a light tug. "I think maybe we should leave," he said.

Aurora pulled firmly away, stooped down and gripped the jukebox power cable where it was plugged into the wall. She yanked it out and killed the music dead.

"Bad idea," whispered Cole.

No one looked at her now. They all turned to the hulking male werewolf with his back to the room, as if waiting for him to act. *The Alpha*, she thought.

"I need to talk with you," said Aurora.

"You need to turn around and run," said the huge male. "Before I rip you to pieces."

Thane.

The voice was unmistakable. Only there was none of the cockiness now. Aurora knew instinctively that he was a different beast to the upstart she had known before. You didn't become Alpha without proving yourself.

"I've come a long way," said Aurora.

Thane slammed his balled fist on to the tabletop, splintering the inch-thick wood. He lurched to his feet, but still didn't face her. He seemed to have grown taller – Aurora thought he matched her six foot five and maybe some more. "I don't give a damn if you've come ten thousand miles. This is my pack, Cage. And you're not welcome."

He didn't need to say anything more for the others to get the message. They began to close in.

"There's no need for that, Thane," said Cole. "She's no threat."

"Shut your mouth, ol'-timer," said Thane. "I'll deal with you later."

"I came because werewolves are dying," said Aurora quickly. As she spoke, she assessed the threat. Four werewolves, one with a pool cue. Barmaid reaching for something under the counter. Shotgun, maybe. She'd come unarmed – even she couldn't sneak a Smith & Wesson through customs. "Someone is trying to awaken Draka."

That made the werewolves pause. In Aurora's estimation, most of them hadn't been around back then, but they'd obviously heard of the Soul Hunter. That sort of thing didn't get forgotten quickly.

Thane bristled too. "You have twenty seconds," he said. "Speak your piece."

"Someone's implanting werewolves with cybernetics to control them," she said. "They came to England, looking for the coin. Beecher and Tanner, and others I didn't know."

The werewolves began to look at one another, frowning. One of the pool players spoke.

"They went missing with Clara, months back," he said.

"We found Clara, but she was already dying," said another – a man holding a cue, with a grubby sleeveless vest and a gut hanging over oil-stained jeans. "She had a wound to the back of her neck. She said she'd escaped from some sort of lab."

"What happened to Beecher and Tanner?" asked Thane.

"Dead," said Aurora, without flinching.

The barmaid's hand went to her mouth. "No!" she cried. *A girlfriend of one, maybe.*

"We need to track down who's doing this," said Aurora.

"No, *we* don't," said Thane. "You ain't one of us any more. And that means you're an enemy."

"Don't be a fool," said Aurora, her patience snapping.

Thane spun round. His face was the same, but his eyes were deadly. Experienced. He'd seen a lot since that day fighting Draka in the bayou. Any trace of greenness, or cowardice, had vanished.

"It's my pack, Cage. You ran away. You don't just get to march in here and start bossing people around." He reached under his shirt and Aurora saw a long dagger sheathed on his belt. No messing around.

"All right," she said, holding up her hands. "We're going."

Thane drew the dagger – it looked freshly sharpened, with wicked serrations on the inside edge all the way to the tip. Gouges to let the blood. "Too late for that," he said. He nodded at the rest of the pack. "She doesn't get outta here alive."

Aurora raised an arm as the man with the pool cue swung at her head. It snapped in the middle, the broken end spinning across and hitting the wall. Aurora grabbed his vest at the collar and yanked him towards her, driving her forehead down. His nose crunched under the force and he fell back, wailing. Two more leapt past her, landing on Cole and smashing through the screen door and down the steps.

The barmaid had a sawn-off shotgun, so Aurora gave her something to think about, grabbing a chair and tossing it across the bar. The girl ducked as glass bottles showered down. Thane pounced with the knife, and Aurora felt the blade slash her arm. She dropped into a spinning sweep and took his legs out from under him.

From outside came snarls and growls. Cole didn't deserve to get caught up in this.

Something landed on Aurora's back, and she felt stabbing pain in her shoulders. She'd forgotten about the other female. She was digging long nails under Aurora's clavicle. Aurora grunted, reached over, and got a handful of hair. She heaved the attacker over her head and threw her down on to her back on the pool table. Balls scattered across the bar's floorboards.

Thane was up again, fast. "No more play-fighting," he said.

"Move!" shouted the barmaid.

Behind the Alpha, Aurora saw the shotgun levelled right at her. Thane moved, and Aurora shifted too, keeping him in the line of fire. She could see the barmaid wasn't sure, and backed away towards the door. The noise outside had died, but she didn't know what that meant.

The girl on the pool table was groggily shaking her head, the one with the bloody nose on all fours.

Suddenly, Cole burst in, fists curled and knuckles bleeding.

The gun went off with a bang, and everyone ducked, Cole included. The jukebox exploded.

Aurora had seen enough. She grabbed Cole's arm and hauled him back outside. The two werewolves he'd been fighting lay on the ground, not moving. Aurora jumped on to her bike and revved the throttle, just as Thane and the others jumped down the steps.

"This isn't over!" Aurora shouted. Her wheels sprayed dirt as she and Cole raced away.

CHAPTER 10

The Stein Foundation, Devon

Evelyn stood by the window, flicking through a thick tome.

Luke tried to remain focused on the trawl. He wished more than ever that his own father were at his side, advising and encouraging. When he'd been a boy, struggling with some question of mathematics or science, Victor Frankenstein always had a way of guiding him through, offering just enough help that Luke thought he'd solved the problem himself.

But as he sorted through various documents, he felt his hope fading. The words of Brother Pietr Domicus still echoed through his brain.

. . . a vampire suffering thus may choose to end his or her time

on the Earth by their own hand, or one close may take pity and commit the final act on their behalf.

Evelyn had stopped crying several minutes ago, and Luke had managed to persuade her to continue the search. But her eyes had taken on a glassy look, and Luke was worried she was losing faith, resigning herself to the inevitable. *There has to be a way*, thought Luke. *There is always a solution.* The problem was they were running out of time.

The door opened with no warning knock. Dr Pavlovic strode in wearing a business suit and white blouse. She was followed by a security team, all stony-faced, wheeling several metal trolleys stacked with plastic boxes.

"What's going on?" asked Evelyn, spinning around.

Dr Pavlovic's eyes passed over them but she didn't reply. Instead, she pointed to the shelves. "I want it all packed up for storage. Label it as best you can."

The men began to move to the shelves.

"Wait!" said Luke. "What do you think you're doing? This is my father's stuff. We need it here. We're searching for a cure for Harker."

"Don't worry," said Dr Pavlovic. "It will be safely transported. You can search at the new location."

"Where?" asked Luke. One of the men was removing a picture of a water-demon from the wall, looking at it with bewilderment.

Dr Pavlovic finally turned to face Luke and Evelyn

properly. "Wherever you choose to go," she said coldly.

Evelyn looked confused and angry. "Don't you understand? We haven't got much time!" she said.

"Miss Harker," the doctor addressed her. "Last night your team were attacked by several . . . intruders, within the Foundation's grounds. And it's clear there could be another attack at any second. I cannot allow my staff to be put at risk. It's only reasonable that you and your associates leave this place forthwith."

"It's completely *un*reasonable," said Evelyn, squaring up. "What about my dad?"

"He can stay until he gets . . . until his illness reaches its conclusion," said Dr Pavlovic. "He'll receive the best possible care."

"I'm not giving up on him," said Evelyn. "Luke owns this place. It's his house. *You* are his employee, a pen-pusher who—"

One of the security staff pulled open the curtain and dawn light seeped into the room. Evelyn was protected from sunlight by a special vaccine, but she still jumped back instinctively.

"Luke, tell her!" said Evelyn. "Just give the order – stop them. Or I might have to do it myself."

Dr Pavlovic glared at Luke. He was seething too, but he managed to gather himself. He certainly didn't feel like the boss, and he was pretty sure most of the staff here wouldn't go against Dr Pavlovic without good reason. They couldn't afford to go to war with the Foundation. He needed them on-side.

"I have a compromise," he said.

"You do?" said Dr Pavlovic.

Evelyn opened her mouth to say something but Luke held up a hand. "Send all non-essential staff away," he said.

"I'm sorry, what?" she replied. "The Foundation can't just—"

"Tell them we're doing essential maintenance," said Luke.

"But how long—"

"Just a few days," he replied.

Dr Pavlovic's lips pursed tightly. She wasn't ready to give in.

"Look," Luke said, losing patience. "We need to save Harker! You may not approve of the Immortals but we're the only ones who can stop the werewolves. There are going to be more. And we need Harker. You may think you're in charge here, and I can see you're doing a good job. But Evelyn's right – this whole place belongs to my family. I don't want to have to shut the place down to prove a point. Help us, and we'll be gone as soon as we can."

Dr Pavlovic breathed deeply through her nose. "Very well," she said at last. With a curt nod, she and the security personnel all left the room.

After the door had closed again, Evelyn slammed her fist into the wall, leaving a huge dent in the plaster.

"Calm down," said Luke. "We need to concentrate on the research. Don't let Pavlovic get to you." But he was starting to have his suspicions about the doctor. She hadn't wanted them here from the start. She must have known this was the safest place for them to be, with access to all the tech and medical equipment.

And come to think of it, how *had* the werewolves known they had come to Devon, without someone tipping them off? Had the doctor been betraying them all along? Would she do anything to make sure the Immortals, and Luke, were out of the way? They weren't safe here. And wherever Aurora was, she wasn't safe either. Pavlovic could have hidden a tiny GPS tracker on all of them.

Luke shook his head. He was getting paranoid. He slumped into his father's leather chair.

His eyes drifted around the study, as if occupying his father's seat might give some kind of insight. His gaze came to rest on the painting over the fireplace – a mountainous landscape below a stormy sky. Swirling oils. Luke thought it might have been Switzerland, where Victor had been from, and where he had married Luke's mother. On either side of the picture were two gilt sconces for holding candles, though both were empty. Luke's heart quickened.

"You look like you've seen a ghost," said Evelyn.

"Maybe I have," said Luke. He wandered towards the fireplace. "Back in our house in London, Dad kept John in a secret room when we had visitors."

"I'm not surprised," said Evelyn.

John was the name Victor had given to his creation – the man he'd put together and resurrected from the dead. Evelyn was right. The scars covering his pale body had given him a ghoulish appearance – not that it had ever bothered Luke. He'd been brought up with John, and saw the giant as an older brother, until the horrible day John had been killed in a battle at the British Museum.

"The entrance to the room," he said. "It was behind a wall." He reached up and wrapped his hand around the left sconce. "To open it, you had to tug one of these."

He jerked the sconce down and a shower of plaster dust fell to the floor. Luke coughed and shook the debris from his hair. "Sorry – I forget my own strength sometimes."

Evelyn managed a laugh. "Good try, though."

Luke was undeterred. He crossed to the other sconce and tugged that one more gently. It rotated on a hidden hinge and hope flared in his chest. He twisted it some more until it went loose in his hand and a dull *thunk* sounded in the wall. The bookshelf beside it opened up an inch.

"There is something!" he said to Evelyn.

She rushed over and helped push the edge of the shelves. They opened like a heavy door.

But what he found on the other side deflated him in an instant. It wasn't a room at all – just a cupboard with a few ink pots, spare quills, and a single large notebook resting on a shelf, caked in dust.

"Is this it?" said Evelyn, shoulders slumping.

Despite his disappointment, Luke had a strange feeling of apprehension in his gut.

"Why go to all that bother just for one book?" he said. "It must be important."

Evelyn picked it up, wiping off a layer of dust with one hand. "Let's find out."

They backed into the main room, and Luke closed the door behind them. It really was a very well-concealed hiding place. He wondered if Dr Fontaine knew of it. Probably not. Which meant the book had lain here, untouched, for over a century.

Evelyn coughed and laid the book on the table, opening the blank front over.

Victor's handwriting covered the inside page:

Theories and Experiments in Immortality Transference.

The title sent a shiver down his spine. Transferring immortality? Surely that wasn't possible – but if it was, it might hold some kind of possibility for Harker. It might be the only way. Luke turned again, and he and Evelyn began to pore over the text.

Luke scanned the first few pages, text about the activity of vampires and werewolves and undead flesh-eaters. Victor had seemed particularly interested in how an immortal could either kill their victim, or "turn" them. In the case of vampires, it seemed to be that a vampire could choose to confer the curse with a non-lethal bite, only partially draining the victim. With werewolves it was a case of the extent of the physical damage. Just a bite would be enough to create a new werewolf, but too great a mauling would simply kill the human. With the undead flesh-eaters – or "zombies", as Evelyn called them – the transferral of powers required merely blood and saliva contact.

While the mechanisms of transferral seem clear enough, all instances incur obvious detrimental side effects. In the case of vampirism, the victim must abandon his moral scruples and become a murderous blood-sucker. The werewolf too loses control under the light of the full moon. The undead walker loses his mind entirely, governed forthwith only by the unsavoury object of human flesh ...

But what if it were possible to confer the benefits of immortality – strength, regenerative abilities, permanent youth – without the deleterious side effects?

A tingle travelled down his spine, as the truth dawned on him. "Dad wanted to become immortal!" said Luke in amazement.

"Just like you did," said Evelyn, meeting his eye for a second with a hint of a smile, before returning to the text.

Next came early experiments on what must have been John, though the creation was as yet unnamed. Both he and Evelyn were silent as they scoured the text.

How frustrating that I am so close to creating a man blessed with immortality, but cannot enjoy the fruits of my work myself!

I have considered investigating the world of witchcraft. I know of those – such as Dodger – who through some curse will live for ever, but as a man of science I am loath to pursue this course. There MUST be a method, a theorised and tested method, to repeat these effects and confound this meagre lifespan allotted to us.

Luke could almost sense his father's insistence in the blotted, hastened letters on the page. As he turned again, he was confronted with a double-spread diagram. Two bodies, side by side, connected with several tubes. More wires trailing off them, and several symbols for laboratory equipment. The bodies were labelled "*Homo Vampyricus*" and "*Homo Sapiens*".

It looked, to Luke, like some sort of blood transfusion – a medical science first practised in the sixteenth century – only much more complicated.

Beneath the diagram was written "Immortality Transferral by Electro-Transfusion – an experiment".

"Do you think he actually tried that?" said Evelyn.

"I have no idea," said Luke. He turned the page. Here there were several dated entries from January 1843.

9 January. My new friend Mr Barker has agreed to take part. Like myself, he is a man of science, working as a physician before he became a vampire himself. He is unconvinced by my method, but in all honesty, so am I. However, as long as we follow strict safeguards, no harm should come to either of us. The date is set for two nights hence. A storm is expected, and we must harvest nature's power to drive the apparatus. I will send Elizabeth away for a few days to stay with her aunt in Kent. If she knew what I was attempting, she would surely try to deter me.

"That explains why the book's hidden away," said Evelyn.

Luke didn't like to think of his father lying to his mother. But there it was in black and white – in Victor's own hand. He read on.

11 January. It is now three hours since the initial stages concluded. As expected, the storm flashed across the moors. We had some trouble locating enough veins in my limbs, and I am sore from being pricked like a pincushion. Barker was serene through the process. Soon the blood was flowing between our bodies. There was pain – a great deal – as the power surged between us. It is my hope that some essence of his vampirism, stimulated by the same electricity which brought John into this world, will awaken in my body. I try to maintain my equilibrium, aware of how one's own mind is the least objective witness, but already I feel ... different.

12 January, before dawn. It has worked! To hell with equilibrium. I have proof! The cuts across my body where the various conduits were attached have all but healed in a matter of hours. It was only when removing the bandages to re-dress the wounds that I discovered it. Barker sleeps still, exhausted by the experiments, but I cannot rest. I will use these hours to note further observations ...

13 January. With Barker's blessing, we repeated the experiments, almost draining the capacitor. The effects are myriad. In addition to the healing my body had undergone, my skin and hair have greater lustre. I am able to run faster, jump higher, see and hear with greater

acuity. In terms of negative side effects, thus far I have yet to isolate a single one. Any concerns about sensitivity to sunlight, or lust for blood, have not been borne out.

15 January. Feeling wretched. We have curtailed the experiments and I am full of shame. While monitoring changes to my own physiology, I neglected to pay close attention to my dear friend. It seems that the transferral of immortal powers is deleterious to the donor. Being a stoic individual, Jonathan did not at first attribute his weakness to anything more than the loss of blood. But it is undeniable. As I gain more powers, he is losing them. The primary evidence was the tardiness of his own healing. Cuts which would typically restore in a matter of seconds are still scabbed a day later. Tests reveal he is becoming weaker also – both his speed and strength have suffered. We must be vigilant in the coming days. If I have caused some irreparable damage to my dear friend, I will be deeply sorry.

25 January. I am pleased to say that Barker has recovered to hale and hearty health. Sadly, any vestiges of the powers I enjoyed have vanished, leaving me feeling weak-bodied. To have tasted such miracles only to have them stripped away seems cruel, but until I can design some new experimental method, I close this chapter of my work. Elizabeth returns tomorrow, and normal life must resume.

The rest of the pages in the book were blank.

"I actually remember all this," said Evelyn. "My dad left me with a governess while he came down here. He never explained exactly why." She turned to Luke, eyes wide. "But can it help us?"

Luke flicked back to the diagram. He tried to think. An idea was floating around the edges of his consciousness, just out of reach. He stared at the image of the two bodies, connected.

"To think, your dad nearly stole my dad's powers," said Evelyn.

Luke clicked his fingers. "That's it!" he said.

"What's what?" replied Evelyn.

"Stealing powers," said Luke. "Your dad's dying. He's lost his regenerative powers. He's effectively become mortal."

Evelyn frowned. "Yeah?"

"But what if he could take someone else's powers?" He pointed at the page. "Like this! We could cure him."

Evelyn rubbed her temple. "But whose?" she said. "I can't see any of the others giving up their immortality. I wouldn't ask them to."

"There's something we don't have to ask," said Luke. "Something so powerful it could definitely cure him."

Evelyn gasped. "Draka's Blood Armour!"

"Exactly," said Luke. "Aurora said it had almost infinite regenerative powers, right?"

Evelyn paced the room. "So we find the Blood Armour, hook it up to a load of cables and then charge it with lightning while we transfer its blood to Dad." She stopped and ran her fingers through her hair. "But we'll have to find the body – and at best Dad's got twenty-four hours left. And we'll have to wait for a storm. We won't have time."

"Aurora knows where the Blood Armour is buried," said Luke excitedly. "And we don't need lightning. Dad was working in the early days of electricity, but now it's ... well, it's everywhere ... "

Evelyn's eyes lit up. "Yes! We've got a chance."

They locked the hidden compartment and, with the book in his satchel, Luke hurried back to the labs. He tried not to think about Dr Pavlovic's hostility – he could deal with her later. This was more important. He wondered if there was a way to get in touch with Aurora.

They reached the door of the infirmary, and pushed it open. Dodger sat on the floor, bent over. Raziel was by the window, looking for all the world like a statue. Dr Fontaine was adjusting a drip, but, from his strained face, Luke could tell things weren't looking good.

"How is he?" asked Evelyn, walking straight to her father's side. Harker looked like a different person altogether. The flesh had withered from his shoulders and neck. His features were sallow, the skin stretched over his cheekbones and forehead. His eyes were closed but every now and then they clenched tightly like he was having a nightmare.

Dr Fontaine pursed his lips and frowned. "I'm afraid he doesn't have long. I'm so sorry, Miss Harker, but you might want to say your goodbyes."

Evelyn took a deep, shuddering breath.

Luke stepped forwards with the book. "We think we may have found something," he said. "Look at this."

Dr Fontaine's frown deepened as he scanned the pages. "This is nineteenth-century medicine," he said. "And sketchy at best. I don't see how it can—"

And then Evelyn screamed.

Harker's eyes had flicked open, bloodshot and wild. One hand snapped up, tearing free of the restraint, and grabbed his daughter by the hair.

"Dad! Stop!" Evelyn shouted.

Harker's body twisted, and his mouth opened, revealing pale gums and long incisors. He sank his teeth into his daughter's neck.

Evelyn cried out in pain and pulled away, shoving Harker back on the bed. His spine stiffened as if he was being electrocuted, the veins across his arms bulging. Then he sagged back, head flopping sideways.

The heart monitor began a high-pitched whine. Luke saw the spiking pulse line had flattened out.

"No!" said Evelyn. "Help him!"

Dr Fontaine went straight to a set of defibrillator pads, as Luke stepped forwards and ripped open Harker's hospital gown at the chest. The vampire's torso was still bruised and stitched from the fight against the werewolves, and painfully malnourished.

"Step aside," said Dr Fontaine.

Dodger and Raziel, who had moved closer, backed away. Everyone looked on.

The defibrillator beeped to indicate full charge and Dr Fontaine held the pads against Harker's chest. With a bang, Harker jerked. Luke looked to the monitor. Still flat.

The machine began to charge again. Fontaine repeated the shock.

No change.

Blood trickled between Evelyn's fingers as she cradled the wound to her neck. She was staring at her father's face, lips slightly parted.

Another shock. Harker twitched wildly, muscles completely limp. Luke willed him to come back. To open his eyes. For the heart monitor to spike into life again.

Fontaine repeated the procedure six, maybe seven times, before he stepped back, the pads held limp in his hands.

"Don't stop!" said Evelyn.

Dr Fontaine looked at her sadly and shook his head. "He's gone, Miss Harker."

"Do it again!" she said. Rounding the bed, she snatched the paddles. "Charge it!"

Dr Fontaine didn't move. No one did. Luke saw Evelyn's shirt collar stained with fresh blood, trailing from two neat puncture wounds above her clavicle. *Homo vampyricus* clotted much more quickly than a normal human. They'd heal in seconds.

Evelyn looked at each of them, and the pain in her eyes was too much to bear.

"I'm sorry," said Dr Fontaine. "There was nothing we could do."

Evelyn began to sob. Luke could hardly believe it. Jonathan Harker – dead. The man who'd defeated Count Dracula. The scientist who'd given Luke a second life. Their leader. He felt tears coming to his own eyes.

"He fought hard," Dodger muttered.

"Dad?" said Evelyn, leaning over Harker. "Dad, wake up. Please."

Harker's eyes were still open a fraction, and Raziel reached out a stone hand. With a gentle touch, he pressed the eyelids closed.

"It's over, Evelyn," he said.

Evelyn turned from the body and buried her head into Raziel's chest. He folded a wing across her back.

For a time the room was silent, then the door opened and Dr Pavlovic stood there. "What's happened?"

Evelyn flashed her tear-stained eyes at the new arrival. "He's dead. Happy now?"

The doctor looked aghast. "Miss Harker," she said at last. "You have my deepest, deepest condolences."

"Save it," said Dodger.

"If you think that I wanted—" said Anna.

"I think you should go," said Dodger. In an instant he was up, holding open the door for Dr Pavlovic. The doctor nodded curtly, and left the room.

Dr Fontaine went to a shelf and unwrapped a dressing. He offered it to Evelyn.

She looked at it for a second.

"For your neck," he said.

Evelyn took it and held it to the wound with a wince.

Luke felt a twinge of unease in his gut. "I need to get back to the study," he said, moving towards the door.

"Now?" said Evelyn.

Luke's eyes were fixed on the dressing she clutched to her neck. A few drops of blood had already seeped through. That wasn't right. Luke felt short of breath, his mind reaching for something else he'd read in the Domicus treatise. He wasn't sure, but . . .

"I have to go," he said.

And then he was running, along the corridors and through the house. He rushed past a few employees, who watched him pass with open mouths.

Luke crashed through the study door, almost knocking it from its hinges. *The Physiology of Vampires* remained on the desk, and his fingers flew over the pages, tearing one in his haste. That didn't matter. All that mattered was ...

His eyes fell on a section of writing, underlined for emphasis. His mind translated, and with every word, dread stole over his heart.

Be aware of contagion. A vampire suffering terminal blood denial must be quarantined. His bite or infected blood can pass the disease to others of his kind ...

Luke read it again, feeling the colour drain from his face. Harker was contagious. He had bitten his daughter. That meant—

A noise in the doorway made him turn around. Evelyn stood there, eyes red-rimmed, the bandage still pressed against her bleeding throat.

CHAPTER 11

Louisiana

"Well, that was fun," said Cole. "You sure know how to make friends, don't you?"

They'd pulled up by the side of the highway, a couple of miles from the bar. Through his ripped jeans, Aurora saw Cole was bleeding from a leg wound. And from the kink in the top of his nose, she guessed it was broken.

"You'll heal," said Aurora, looking at the cuts where the other werewolf's nails had sliced her shoulder. "But hey, thanks for backing me up."

Cole shrugged. "I never liked Thane much. Pity you didn't rip him to pieces."

Aurora grinned. Her jaw ached and she realised she must have been punched at some point. Truth was, much as she'd have liked to kill Thane, he was a different animal now. She *might* still be able to take him, but it wouldn't be an easy fight.

"What now?" said Cole. "I guess we're on our own."

Aurora pondered. "Do you know where Tanner and Beecher were last seen? Could be a good place to start."

Cole shrugged. "At the clubhouse with Thane, I think. But I know they found Clara south-east of here, near Gheens. Storm came in, though. Her scent was washed away. No hope of tracking where she might have come from."

Aurora nodded. She scanned the clear blue sky to the horizon. There was one more possibility she could think of. A place where they might find a lead. But she wasn't at all sure she was ready to go back there. "Whoever got Tanner and the others was after me, right?"

"That's what it sounds like."

"I know a place where they might have looked for me," she said.

"You do?" said Cole. "It's all changed since you were last here."

"We'll see," she replied. "Follow me."

She kicked back the bike's stand, and let the engine growl, heading back on to the highway with Cole. They headed south over the dead flat landscape, until the curvature of the Earth hid all of New Orleans from view.

She was glad Cole wasn't a talker – she needed time to think. She opened the throttle and let the breeze blast her.

Something about the whole encounter at the bar didn't feel right. Thane was a thug, but he wasn't dumb. Why hadn't he even wanted to listen about Tanner and Beecher? In fact, she didn't even think he'd registered surprise on hearing they were dead. He'd seemed paranoid. She wondered if he knew more than he was letting on. Hiding something, maybe? Cole had said that Thane was the last one to see them alive . . .

After three-quarters of an hour, they cut on to a smaller track. Even though the roads had changed, her nose told her the way, and with every mile they covered, her heart grew a little heavier.

Eventually, they pulled up outside a crumbling house. The huge ironwood that had stood in the front yard was dead – split by lightning by the looks of it – but others had grown up around it. The outbuilding had blown down some time in the last one hundred and seventy years. But the house was the same as she remembered. Sure, the windows were gone or broken, and the veranda was sprouting an array of plants, but that was just cosmetic.

"Where the hell are we?" said Cole.

Aurora sighed. "Home," she said.

Cole didn't say anything.

"Keep your guard up," said Aurora.

They left the bikes on the track, and climbed over the remains of the low picket fence. The grass was knee high, but some of the vegetation was broken. Maybe raccoons, or something bigger.

Aurora went first. The front steps creaked under her weight. She spied animal droppings on the veranda, and the front door was a little ajar.

Aurora eased it further open with her fingertips. The interior smelt musty, but she couldn't detect any fresh trail. If someone had come here it wasn't for a while.

She heard Cole enter behind her. "Can't smell anyone," he whispered.

Aurora sniffed again. There was another scent lingering. Something chemical that didn't sit right at all.

"This must have been a nice place," said Cole.

"It was," said Aurora. She couldn't tell if he was trying to be funny.

There was little sign of that now, though. The wooden floorboards were cracked and rotting with damp, the furniture just as bad, sprouting mould. More droppings. A couple of old watercolours hanging at angles on the walls. Aurora ignored the flashes of memory from the fateful day, and focused instead on happier times. She'd grown up here, a happy, regular childhood with her brother Hector. Playing hide and seek in the house's many nooks and crannies.

Fishing in the large pond out back. Running in when her mom called her for dinner. After their folks had passed on, Hector and Aurora took on the place together.

"We need to look around," said Aurora. "If someone came here looking for me, they might have left a clue." She walked across the groaning floor and peered into the simple country kitchen, with its cast-iron range covered in cobwebs and rust. Weeds sprouted under the back door and the window frames had rotted down to almost nothing, the glass sagging and distorted.

Life had all changed when they got into a row over land with the neighbouring plantation owner, Dupree. He challenged Heck to a duel, but Aurora knew Dupree was a crafty son of a gun, and since Hector had a wife and a kid on the way, and Aurora had always been the brawler, she'd taken her brother's place, locking him in the basement and dressing in his clothes. It was night when they were due to settle things, so no chance the sheriff might be out. Aurora, huge and broad, had no trouble passing for a man. In fact, people were usually keen to avoid her.

And it all would have been well, if it hadn't been for the full moon. Because Dupree was even craftier than she'd guessed. Turned out he was a werewolf.

She'd got the fright of her life when she faced him at Gunther's Ford, and he started to sprout hair, dropping to all fours. The pistol had no effect, and his teeth were in her arm before she could even reload. The only thing that saved her was her pa's old dagger, which she kept in her boot. She'd jammed it through Dupree's eyeball, not knowing its hilt was solid silver. Took her half an hour to squeeze out from under his dead body, and even then she'd no idea what it meant.

The next full moon had been an unpleasant surprise.

Even after she'd been turned, and her life became that of a wanderer, she'd come back often to see Hector's family. Her beautiful niece and nephew, Europa and Lysidas. She remembered telling them stories by the fire.

Aurora tried to dispel the memories, and scanned the room for any sign it had been searched. Some kitchen drawers were pulled out and one of the cupboard doors hung open. Piles of broken china scattered the floor. She continued on and came upon the hearth. Now it was black and empty, the poker rusty and leaning in its stand. On a full moon she'd steered well clear of her folks, but other times, this house was always a haven where she could feel normal again. Almost.

At the bottom of the rickety stairs, she paused. Another waft of that chemical smell. She looked down and saw there was half a footprint in the thick dust on the ground. "Someone's been here," she said. The banister was scuffed too. A few more footmarks further up the steps.

"How recent?" Cole asked.

"Not long ago, I'd guess," she said. "Otherwise the prints would have faded." She looked up the steps, wondering what she'd find. She couldn't sense anyone else in the house, but it wouldn't be the first time her nose had let her down. She went to the fireplace and grabbed the poker.

"I'll go first," she said in a whisper.

Cole nodded, drawing a flick-knife.

They headed upstairs slowly, and Aurora tried to resist the tide of memories. Running up and down, the bunk in her room, shooting her first rifle at quail from the window. The state of the place almost brought her to tears, but she focused instead on the signs of intruders. In her folks' old room, there were fingerprints on dressers, wardrobe doors flung open, old moth-eaten sheets and clothes strewn on the ground. Then she turned back into the corridor and stood facing the final room. She didn't want to go inside. Not yet.

But she knew she had to.

She stared at the door, chills rippling over her skin, fingers curled tight around the poker. Then with a sharp breath, she forced herself to enter the room that had belonged to Lysidas and Europa.

Empty.

Inside, Aurora fell against the bedroom wall, fighting

back the sudden surge of almost unbearable loss. Their bunk remained, a few toys scattered around the floor, wooden trains and a moth-eaten teddy bear. She looked at the spot under the shredded curtains where she'd found them. She remembered how she'd scrubbed the floorboards for hours to get rid of the blood.

Aurora clenched her fists, nails pressing into her palms. She swore to herself that if someone was trying to bring back the demon that had killed her family, she wouldn't stop until she had tracked them down.

She felt Cole's hand on her shoulder. "Cage?"

"I'm fine," she said. She pointed to a loose floorboard ripped up.

"They were definitely looking for something," said Cole.

"And they weren't worried about being discreet," said Aurora. Her hand went automatically to her pocket, before remembering that Luke had the coin.

Cole sniffed.

"You smell it too?" she said.

He nodded. "Chemicals. Hard to make out. Iodine is one of them, I reckon. Used for sterilisation."

"Formaldahyde, too," said Aurora. She recognised it from the vat where Luke's body had been preserved, in Southwark Cathedral. She couldn't name the others. But together they reminded her of something. She couldn't think in here though. She paced from the room, down the stairs, and out into the yard. She slumped on to the grass, back resting against the trunk of the blackened ironwood. Cole emerged a few seconds later and crouched beside her.

"I know what the smells remind me of," said Aurora. "Science laboratories."

Cole's eyes went wide. "Clara mentioned a lab."

"Any round here?" asked Aurora.

"Maybe," said Cole. He fished in his jacket, drew out a smartphone and tapped the screen, then turned the display to Aurora. There were several within a couple of hundred miles, but one jumped out at her right away – Mindscience. It was located just outside the town of Lockhart. Aurora stared up at Cole, pulse racing.

"This one," said Aurora, pointing to the phone and staring at Cole. "Lockhart. That's about ten miles from Gheens, right? Where Clara was discovered."

Cole's mouth opened slowly. "Yeah . . . Coincidence?"

"I don't believe in them," Aurora replied. She tried to look at the firm's web page, but it no longer existed. "We need to go there, now." She held up her hand to Cole, and he hoisted her to her feet.

"OK," he said. "But we scope it out first. Who knows what we're up against. And I don't fancy getting captured. Don't think I'd suit a brain implant."

"I'm with you on that," said Aurora.

Aurora took a last glance at her old home then headed with Cole through the overgrown garden, back to the bikes. As she turned the key, and the massive engine fired up, the adrenaline began to pulse through her. They were heading into the lions' den. What she wouldn't give to have the Immortals by her side right now.

They rode their bikes past the entrance road, a set of electronic gates visible fifty metres down it. They parked up on the verge a mile away, then kept to the treeline as they made their way back along the freeway by foot. Judging by the aerial shots online, Mindscience was substantial, covering a good few acres. There was nothing within several miles on any side apart from swampland and a freight track running west. "Cheap land," Cole had said.

Or something to hide? Aurora thought.

They came to the entrance road. Looking at the tall grass growing up the side of the track, it seemed no one had set foot out this way for at least a few months.

"Abandoned?" asked Cole.

"Maybe that's what they want people to think," said Aurora. "Stay alert."

They paced down the road, warily. Aurora kept expecting to see huge hairy bodies moving between the trees. But they encountered no one – no guards, no werewolves, no scientists. When they reached the gate, Aurora was surprised to see that it was half open. The security cameras on the fence were dead, too.

Beyond, the main building was single-storey, glass-fronted, and surrounded by pre-fab huts. "Looks deserted to me," said Cole.

Aurora strode forward, but Cole grabbed her arm. "Thought we were scouting it out," he said.

"We just did." She entered through the gate to the lab. The doors were locked up, but Aurora put a boot through one of the panes and they crunched in over broken shards.

A front desk in the reception, computer monitor and keyboard. Paperwork and key cards in a drawer. They vaulted over an automated turnstile, then passed through what seemed to be some sort of defunct body scanner.

If Mindscience was a scientific laboratory, it was nothing like the Stein Foundation in appearance. There were no glass walls here, just a few doors punctuating the long corridors. And there was a different feeling in the air. As if misery lingered in the shadowy corners of the labs, and forgotten screams echoed in between her footsteps.

All the doors had key-card readers, but the electrics were down, so most of the doors were open. Along a main corridor, though, there was a set of metal double doors that was jammed shut. "On three," Aurora said to Cole. After Aurora counted down, they shoulder-charged it and the metal buckled completely. Aurora and Cole stumbled through. Aurora stared round for attackers. But it was quiet. Some sort of admin office with filing cabinets.

Except the stench of stale blood filled the air.

Aurora looked at Cole and he gave her a grim look. "It's coming from that way," she said, pointing to large sliding doors at the end of the room. Beyond, Aurora was surprised to see thick swampland. She approached and opened the doors. Birds squawked and the fetid odour of decaying plant life washed over her. But the stench of blood was underneath it, strong.

There was a lake, maybe fifty metres across, surrounded by the twisted roots of the bald cypress trees. A layer of algae lay across the surface, blocking out the light, killing everything below it.

"Aurora," said Cole. He was crouching ahead by the edge of the bank. She went over. He was bent over a bundle of thick cables running out of the water. "They lead back towards to the building," he said.

They followed them through the dead, overgrown grass, back to the building, where they ran up the outside wall and entered what looked like a locked fuse box.

Aurora smashed her elbow into it and the door swung open. A single button was inside. Aurora glanced at Cole then jammed it down with a finger. A mechanical whine filled the air.

"The swamp," whispered Cole in amazement. Ripples were spreading across the green carpet. Then the lake began to bubble, until it was a roiling torrent of green water.

"I don't believe it," murmured Cole. Something was rising up from the depths. Some kind of huge metal platform, thirty metres wide and half the length of a football field.

Steel walls appeared underneath it. It was some kind of submerged building. There were a few narrow windows in the side. "I think we've found the labs," said Aurora.

"Looks more like a prison," said Cole.

The metal structure groaned. Then it shuddered, and came to a halt.

A metal walkway had risen up, leading from the bank to a thick steel door. Aurora tested it with a foot, then trod across. The scent of blood and decaying flesh filled her nostrils, overpowering even the swamp. Goosebumps prickled her neck, and she could hear Cole's ragged breathing behind her.

Whoosh.

Aurora jumped as the steel door slid to the side, spraying her face with pond water. "Automatic," she said.

Motion-sensitive lights flickered on, revealing a surgical room – but not like a hospital. More like a morgue. The bed wasn't made for comfort – it was just a steel surface. Manacles for ankles and wrists. Chains hanging from the sides. Some sort of magnetic resonance imaging chamber, like a futuristic coffin.

And, above all, the definite smell of werewolf.

Cole looked worried. "What the hell is this place?" he said.

Aurora went through another door into the next room.

Something between a metal shop and a technology lab. Computers everywhere, flat-screen monitors attached to a wall. Wiring, circuit boards, robotics she didn't have the first clue about.

The smell was stronger here, and it turned her stomach.

Cole could smell it too. He was grimacing.

Her gaze fell upon a metal object on a table. Two shining prongs, with bundles of small wires running off them. "A brain implant," said Aurora, picking it up. "Same as the one we found in the wolves on Dartmoor." She threw it back to the table with disgust.

Ahead, another door, this one vacuum-sealed. It gave a hiss as she pushed through, releasing a sickening waft of death.

"Oh no," she breathed.

More like a zoo in here. Cages lining the wall,

compartmentalised. Thick bars that her senses screamed at her not to touch. *Silver.* The stink of decayed faeces and death. Clumps of hair. Blood smears on the walls.

Bones in the corner of a cage. Just a random jumble, and human, by the looks of them. Teeth marks. Shreds of white clothing stained mostly red.

Aurora didn't need to inspect them more closely. "Food," she said, grimly.

Cole's face turned pale as he picked out a tattered and bloody denim jacket from a cage. "Clara's," he said. "She was here."

A picture was forming in Aurora's head even though she wanted to block out the sheer horror. Captured werewolves brought here, interrogated in silver cages. That's how they found out Aurora was in London. Then they were experimented upon, the metal implants inserted into their brains, turned into mindless soldiers.

She walked to the centre of the room, trying to stay detached, trying not to think about Beecher and Tanner and God knows who else trapped in those cages, driven mad by the silver, smashing their heads against the walls and bars in an effort to escape. Tried not to think of the poor humans dragged in to feed them.

It was too much.

She turned, pushing past Cole and hurrying from the room. Past the tech room where the implants were created, through the steel prison chamber and back out into the corridor.

She retched, threatening to empty her guts on a dust-covered carpet.

After a few seconds, she saw Cole's feet. She spat out the taste of bile and wiped her mouth as she stood up. "This is all because of me," she said. "They wanted to get to me. To find out where the coin is. Then they turned the werewolves into their soldiers to come and get it."

"It's not your fault," said Cole. "We need to find out who ran this place." He cracked his knuckles. "When we do, it won't be pretty."

Aurora nodded. "It's clear they'll stop at nothing to get that coin. To use Draka's power somehow." Then a thought sprang up. "There might be records, in the offices from earlier."

They headed back into the main building and into the offices. Aurora began to pull open drawers and filing cabinets. There were purchase orders for scientific equipment, invoices, payroll documents and other boring admin.

She went to a desk and pulled open the top drawer, then froze.

The room seemed to spin a little around her and Aurora had to steady herself against the chair.

"You OK?" asked Cole.

Aurora turned to face him, dangling a key card from the end of a fabric cord. There was a small passport-sized photo on it. A man smiling broadly. He had hair in the picture, and a moustache, but there was no mistaking him.

Dr Fontaine.

CHAPTER 12

The Stein Foundation, Devon

"Are you sure you want to do this?" said Dr Fontaine, as they walked to the elevators. "We could wait a while. Everyone's been through a tough time."

He put a sympathetic hand on Luke's shoulder as they waited for the lift to arrive. Luke couldn't have rested, even if he wanted to. Whenever he let his mind drift, it went back to Harker's corpse in the medical rooms upstairs. He felt empty, defeated. It still didn't seem real.

"I don't know how long Evelyn's got," said Luke. Under his arm he had his father's journal, marked at the page of the transferral experiment. Dr Fontaine had said it might be possible to recreate the equipment, better it even. Luke clung to the hope he was right.

Evelyn herself had insisted she felt no different, and it was true her neck wound *had* finally clotted. But Luke thought he could already see the changes. He'd pointed out that her hair looked less lustrous than normal, her eyes circled beneath with dark rings.

"I'm just tired," she'd replied. "I never thought you paid much attention to a girl's hair."

Luke wasn't taking any chances. He'd told her to remain with her father and the others. Dodger was loading weapons into the Foundation's plane, watched curiously by the pilot the Foundation was providing. If they were going to succeed they needed to find the Blood Armour. They had been trying to call Aurora for its location, but her phone was off. He knew she needed to focus on her own mission. He put his hand to his jacket breast and felt the shape of the coin. He wondered how she was getting on, if she had found anything. Mostly he hoped she got their message soon. Now Evelyn had the illness, who knew how long she would last.

The elevator doors opened and Dr Fontaine smiled at him as he pressed the button for the tech labs, the lift lowering them down. "You seem a little distracted," he said to Luke. "Is something the matter?"

The doors opened on to the expanse of the tech labs, with their workbenches and shelves of equipment. For a moment

Luke thought about revealing the coin to Dr Fontaine, but then he stopped himself. Aurora wouldn't like it. And Luke still had his suspicions about Dr Pavlovic. "Nothing at all," said Luke. He cleared his throat. "So do you think we have everything we need down here?"

Dr Fontaine exited the elevator and gestured with a hand for Luke to follow. "I do hope so."

Luke was surprised to see several scientists already at work, despite the hour. *Maybe they work in shifts down here*, he thought. "I've been looking at Dad's experiment again. I think we could achieve the right voltage with a powerful enough battery . . . " He trailed off.

A strange look had come over Dr Fontaine, and it was clear he wasn't listening. One by one the white-coated scientists in the room turned to face him, setting down what they were working with.

"What's going on?" Luke said.

"I know Aurora's in Louisiana," said Dr Fontaine.

"Oh," said Luke, not sure how to respond. The scientists in the lab were standing in a line watching him, completely still. Something about their glassy-eyed stares seemed familiar, and made Luke feel uncomfortable, his pulse quickening. Why were they all just watching him? He felt suddenly claustrophobic. Then Dr Fontaine nodded beyond Luke's shoulder.

Before he could turn, something pressed into Luke's

side and pain surged through his body. His strength left him and he crumpled to the ground beside a scientist holding a taser. His mind whirred, confused. He squinted at the scientist standing over him. As the white-coated man turned, Luke saw the flash of something metal just above his collar. Terrible realisation crept through Luke. It was an implant. He squinted at the man's fingernails, then at those of the other scientists. They were all tapered like claws. Luke's blood turned to ice. *The scientists are werewolves in human form.*

"Pick him up," said Dr Fontaine coldly.

Hands reached down. Luke played weaker than he felt as the man hoisted him up with ease. Then he turned and drove his lightning blade into the scientist's gut. The man looked down with his lips parted in surprise. Luke kicked him off the blade and across a bench. To his horror, the scientist stood, shakily, on the other side. His face was blank, like a mask.

"Unless that blade is silver – and I know it isn't because I designed it – you'd be better to save yourself a fight," said Dr Fontaine.

Luke felt a jolt of horror. His glance flicked to the elevator. How long until the others came to find him? He'd left them with Harker at the infirmary. He tried desperately to think of a way of contacting them, but panic was seizing hold of him and his brain was foggy from the taser shock.

Dr Fontaine followed his gaze. "They won't come, Luke," he said. "They're too busy with Harker. They won't spare a thought for you. Lucky for me, really." The other white coats closed in.

Luke brandished his blade, but they didn't even hesitate. *Of course not. They're under Fontaine's control.*

Luke slashed one across the arm with the lightning blade, then leapt up on to a table. One jumped up after him, and Luke's foot met his chin with a roundhouse kick. He fell off, dazed but not unconscious. Another grabbed Luke's legs and yanked them back with incredible strength. Luke's face hit the tabletop with a thud and pain exploded across his cheek. More hands seized his limbs. He flailed blindly, but there was no way he could fight off a pack of werewolves, even if they were in human form. Their long nails tore through his clothes, into his skin.

"Flip him over," said Dr Fontaine.

They picked him up and slammed him down again, face up, on to the table. All the air left Luke's lungs.

He gasped, struggling to draw a breath, and looked for Dr Fontaine. The doctor was standing with his arms folded across his chest and a pleased half-smile on his face. His manner and the cruelly determined expression he wore made him appear an entirely different man to the kindly scientist of a few minutes ago: his eyes were glazed, the pupils dilated in a mad, unblinking stare. The harsh laboratory light illuminated thin veins beneath the pale skin on his scalp.

"Kill the elevator," he told one of his assistants. "We don't want to be disturbed." He spoke flatly, without emotion. "Give me the coin, Luke," said Dr Fontaine, without even looking at him. "I've no wish to hurt you."

Luke needed to buy time. "What coin?" he said. He felt like an idiot – he had suspected Dr Pavlovic of betraying them, but it was Dr Fontaine. Dr Fontaine was the one implanting the mind-control tech into the werewolves. He had the know-how. And it explained how the werewolves had managed to ambush the Immortals in Southwark Cathedral without being picked up by BIOS. Dr Fontaine must have hacked the system! It was his creation, after all.

Dr Fontaine flashed a mirthless smile. "Nice try." He pointed to a wall-mounted security camera above the elevator door. "I saw Cage give it to you. Hand it over."

Luke gritted his teeth, about to tell Dr Fontaine to go to Hell, when an idea flashed into his head. "OK," he said. "I'll give it to you. It's in my satchel."

Dr Fontaine's eyes were burning with hunger. "Get it."

Luke pulled his satchel from his shoulder, and dug around. His fingers found his communications headset. He flicked on the microphone – it would pick up everything said in the room. *I hope one of the others has got a headset nearby.* Then Luke gripped the hard metal of his grappling hook arm attachment. He pulled it out and swung the metal hook, smashing a werewolf in the face. The werewolf crumpled to the floor. He swung at another, and tried to jump clear of them, but the weight of three more white-coated werewolves pinned him down, while another sank its teeth into his wrist. Luke screamed out in pain and dropped the grappling hook.

"Now, now," said Dr Fontaine. "Behave yourself." He nodded to a werewolf. "Search him. Find it."

Hands rooted through Luke's clothes. As one fetched out the coin from Luke's inside pocket, Luke cursed himself for not hiding it. He'd let Aurora down. He hoped desperately that the Immortals had heard what was happening.

The werewolf tossed the coin to Dr Fontaine, who snatched it out of the air. He bit his lip and seemed to hold his breath.

"Thank you," he said. "I've searched a long time for this."

Luke writhed and the hands tightened. "Why?" he asked.

There were six werewolves in the room, and Dr Fontaine. He was sure he was going to die, very soon. His only chance was to keep Dr Fontaine talking, until the Immortals arrived. *If* they were coming at all.

"Come, come," said Dr Fontaine. "Don't play the fool with me. You know what it is."

"Ten cents?" Luke mumbled.

Dr Fontaine's smile twisted into a cold sneer. "The Soul

Hunter," he said in a breath of awe. He put the coin in his own pocket, then drew out a knife. Luke stiffened, but Dr Fontaine only chuckled. "Don't worry, it's not for you," he said, rolling up his sleeve. "I've got greater plans for the immortal son of Victor Frankenstein."

Luke flinched as Dr Fontaine dragged the tip of the knife across his own forearm, slicing deep into the skin. Blood welled in the gash and dribbled down Dr Fontaine's hand and fingers. He grimaced, but let it spill on to the floor, walking in a circle and moving his hand so the dripping blood made a shape. He bent down and, with a finger, smeared the droplets into a seven-pointed star about two metres across. He clicked his fingers again and another werewolf stepped forwards with a bandage and wrapped it several times around the wound. The rest remained motionless, their expressions blank and the pupils of their eyes dilated. Fontaine rolled down his sleeve. He tossed the knife aside. Blood began to soak his doctor's coat almost at once.

"You don't know what you're doing," said Luke, filled with disgust.

"BIOS, solution 41-X, please," said Dr Fontaine.

Across the lab, one of the cabinets opened, revealing a single stoppered test tube. One of the werewolves who wasn't holding Luke went to retrieve it.

"Why are you doing this?" asked Luke.

"I dedicated years to the study of the brain," said Fontaine. "My father died of a brain tumour, his father too. It goes back a long way in my family. And now at last—" he tapped his gleaming cranium "—now it has come for me." He bent down, showing a scar on the top of his head surrounded by a bald patch. "Surgeons tried to operate, but it wasn't possible to remove. And so I began to experiment with other ways to prolong life, such as extracting werewolf immortality."

Luke felt anger rage inside him. "Against their will! You're supposed to be a *scientist*!"

"So was your father," said Dr Fontaine emphatically. "I draw much inspiration from him."

Luke shook his head slowly. "You're nothing like my father."

For a moment Dr Fontaine's lips quivered in a smile, then his jaw clenched and he jabbed a finger at Luke. "He too was captivated by immortality! He too wanted to conquer death!" His eyes were wide and glistening. "That's why I came here in the first place, to gain access to his work. You must understand that desire?"

Luke bit his lip to stop himself protesting. *He wants my approval*, Luke realised. It might give him some more time. "I understand. But why didn't you just get a werewolf to bite you?" asked Luke.

"A crude method," said Dr Fontaine. "Only one in ten

survive the transformation. But it didn't matter. By then some had confessed to me about the existence of Draka, the Soul Hunter. A creature of incredible power! And I had the perfect foot soldiers at my disposal. Again, it was your father that inspired me! I read about Aurora's serum, how it could manipulate the chemistry of a werewolf's brain. But I went much further ... I created mind-control technology!" Dr Fontaine threw out his arms dramatically. Then he brandished the coin. "And now I have him, and immortality is in my grasp."

He placed the silver dime on the ground in the middle of the star of blood.

Where are the others? Luke wondered desperately. *They must be close by now.* Dr Fontaine clicked his fingers. The werewolf handed the test tube to him.

"You can't be serious," said Luke. "How will releasing Draka help you? He'll kill us all."

"That's what the runic marking is for," said Dr Fontaine, pointing to the star. "I found it in one of your father's books. It will contain him, until he does my bidding."

"You hope," said Luke. "This isn't science. It's dark magic."

Dr Fontaine looked momentarily uncertain. Then he took out the stopper on the test tube, and leaned over the coin. Slowly, he poured out a trickle of the clear liquid. As the liquid made contact with the coin, the nickel and silver amalgam began to hiss and melt away in a swirl of pinkish smoke.

Luke heard a distant voice calling. It sounded like Evelyn. His heart raced. Dr Fontaine glanced towards the elevator, then poured more quickly, and the acid splashed across the floor.

With a tremendous crash, the elevator doors buckled. A stone hand prised through the crack. Then another.

Raziel!

The doors separated slowly, and Luke saw Dodger and Evelyn. They burst into the room, straight for Dr Fontaine and the mystic star. *If they break it . . .*

"No, wait!" cried Luke. "Stay back!"

The Immortals halted as the smoke arising from the coin swirled and flashed with light and Dr Fontaine stepped back. The werewolves looked on blankly.

"Draka, awaken!" Dr Fontaine cried. "Witness the one who has freed you from captivity. Bless me with everlasting life and I will let you hunt again."

The smoke spun in a column, but in its depths thrashed an indistinct liquid shape, like a web of glistening scarlet tissue strands throwing themselves against an invisible wall, searching for a way to escape.

"What do we do?" asked Evelyn.

The smoke began to seep out from the star, and Luke saw why. "The acid!" he shouted.

Dr Fontaine looked down and his face contorted in terror.

Part of the star had burned away. "That's not supposed to happen!" cried Dr Fontaine, backing off.

As the narrow trail of smoke escaped, it gathered in the air like a ball of raw red flesh. It paused for a moment, pulsing slightly like a malformed heart, then slammed into Dr Fontaine's chest, disappearing into the scientist. He folded into a ball, grunting and crying out. Luke had no idea what Draka's spirit was doing to him, but from the terrible choking sounds he guessed it was painful.

Dr Fontaine suddenly straightened, trembling from head to toe, his eyes closed.

"That don't look good," said Dodger.

Dr Fontaine's eyes shot open and Luke swallowed. His eyes were bright red, as if all the blood vessels had burst at once. He opened his mouth and spoke, but the voice was not Dr Fontaine's. It was rasping, deep and ageless, and it sent shivers along Luke's spine.

"Where is the Blood Armour?"

Evelyn had drawn her staff and flipped it to full length. She pointed the spiked tip at Dr Fontaine.

"What's happening to him?"

"I think Draka has taken over," said Luke.

Dr Fontaine's body paced towards the werewolf who'd given him the acid. He wrapped a hand around her neck and hoisted her off her feet. "Where is it?" For a moment, her eyes too went red and she wailed in pain. "Where is the Blood Armour?" roared Draka's voice.

"The Blind Lagoon, master," croaked the werewolf. Her brain implant clearly forced her to answer to Dr Fontaine. But Luke knew it wasn't Dr Fontaine any more.

It was *Draka*.

The Soul Hunter shook her by the throat. Luke heard the spine snap and she was dropped to the ground.

He turned on the others in the room, his red gaze sweeping over all of them, but resting on Luke. Luke sensed pure evil in the red orbs.

"Your soul is strong," boomed the voice of Draka, as he drifted forward. "Let me feast upon it."

Luke's skin itched with fear as the Soul Hunter approached. The werewolves still held him spreadeagled and powerless. Then something silver slammed into the temple of the one holding his right arm. A silver throwing star. Luke saw Dodger with his arm outstretched. The werewolf loosened its grip and fell back, stiff as a board. Luke severed the hand of another werewolf, then rammed his lightning blade into Draka's chest. The red eyes widened in shock, then he grinned.

Draka moved away, and the lightning blade slid out of his chest, covered in blood. How was he still breathing? It must have gone right through the heart!

"Stop him!" said Luke.

Evelyn spun her staff, and Raziel dropped into a crouch. But Draka casually extended a hand. Blue energy crackled in his fingertips, and then shot forward. Raziel threw out a wing to protect the others. A bright light blinded Luke, making him clamp shut his eyes, and over Raziel's roar of pain he heard Draka's voice.

"Vengeance shall be mine on the human world! A hunt is coming, like nothing before. The cursed city will be my feeding ground, and a reign of death shall be released."

The light died, and Luke opened his eyes to see Raziel on the ground, his shoulder cracked and smoking, revealing the molten orange swirl of his mysterious flesh beneath. Dodger picked himself off the floor, but Evelyn moved weakly. She couldn't take any sort of fight, not in her condition.

"Where'd he go?" groaned Dodger.

Draka was already in the doorway to the emergency stairs. "Kill them all," he commanded.

That blue light . . . Luke thought. *It's the same as Sanakhte's magic was.*

"Evelyn!" he said. "Get away!"

One of the werewolves leapt over the remains of the blood star, claw-like hands outstretched. Luke wasn't quick enough with the lightning blade and the creature slashed his face. Burning pain shocked him to his senses. Luke ducked another swipe, and thrust a foot into the attacker's middle.

It buckled. Luke sidestepped and brought the blade down. The werewolf's head rolled across the floor and a fountain of blood decorated the wall.

More were stalking towards him, and he fumbled for one of the sonic grenades in his satchel. He tripped backwards over a desk and lost his grip, spilling it from his fingers as he landed on his back. A werewolf pounced, feet stamping at Luke's head. Dodger appeared from nowhere, shoving it aside, before leaping up on to a table and smashing a vial. The silver fluoride cloud had the werewolves clawing at their throats, and Dodger moved between them at incredible speed, tripping them with his extendable wire.

Luke scrambled across to where Evelyn lay. She was bleeding from a cut to her cheek, eyelids fluttering.

"We need to get her out of here," he shouted at Raziel.

Despite his injured shoulder, Raziel lumbered upright and scooped Evelyn off the ground, and then leapt across the room to the door to the emergency stairs. With a grunt, he pushed through and disappeared.

Luke faced the werewolves again. One had Dodger by the scruff of the neck, smashing his head repeatedly against a wall.

"Any time—" *SMASH* "—you want to—" *SMASH* "—help."

Luke ran, slid between a werewolf's legs, then sliced upwards with his lightning blade, severing the arm holding

Dodger. The werewolf roared and tried to bite Luke, but just got his jacket. Three more closed in on them. Dodger's head was gushing blood and he was breathing heavily. Luke's face throbbed from the claw wounds. They backed away.

"Think we can take 'em?" asked Dodger.

Luke raised his lightning blade, ready to try.

Then something rattled between his feet, spinning to a stop on the ground between them and the werewolves.

Sonic grenade.

"Cover your ears!" he shouted.

He dived at the same time, but still heard the boom through his hands. When he turned around, all the werewolves were sprawled across the room, stunned. Luke looked towards the elevator, wondering who'd thrown the grenade. Dr Pavlovic was propped up against the elevator open doors, her hair a mess, clutching the pin.

"Not bad for a pen-pusher, don't you think?"

They left the remaining werewolves squirming in a silver net and, with the elevator out of action, climbed the emergency stairs. At the top, they pushed past the crowd of security employees who had gathered in a corridor.

"There's been a breach," panted Dr Pavlovic. "Initiate evacuation procedures."

There were sceptical looks and a barrage of questions, but then everyone was drowned out by the roar of an engine.

Luke broke into a run, bursting out through the main doors to see a small, sleek aeroplane climbing into the sky above the furthest agri-tents. Raziel was flying after it, but he was nowhere near quick enough, and dropped back as it ascended. Evelyn limped over, ashen-faced, and Luke caught her as she fell towards him. Dodger raced up alongside them.

"Draka got away," Evelyn croaked. "In the plane."

Luke spared a thought for the pilot stuck on the aircraft with the Soul Hunter, as he watched the jet break into the low reaches of dusk cloud. Despair filled his heart. And then an unnerving thought wormed its way into his mind. "That blue light Draka fired from his fingers . . ." Luke said. "It was Sanakhte's magic, I'm sure of it." He gazed at Evelyn and Dodger. "Do you think Draka has been absorbing the power of all the supernatural creatures the Immortals and Aurora have killed, while he's been in the coin?"

Evelyn chewed her lip, looking pale. "He'll be unbelievably strong," she whispered. Dodger's eyes were wide.

"Blimey. That's not good," he said.

Worry churned in Luke's stomach. They needed to stop Draka before he got to his Blood Armour or they wouldn't stand a chance against him. They wouldn't be able to save Evelyn. And Draka, more powerful than ever, would have the population of a modern city to feast on. *New Orleans will be a bloodbath.*

"What are we waiting for?" said Dodger. "We've gotta get after him."

Dr Pavlovic arrived too, watching the plane vanish. "What on earth just happened?" she asked. "Was that Gregory?"

Luke looked at her. "That's not Fontaine any more," he said. "It's Draka. And he's gone to retrieve his body."

Dr Pavlovic looked bewildered. "I think you might need to explain a few things."

Luke looked again at the trails left behind by the jet. They knew where Draka was going. All wasn't lost. "OK," he said. "But first, we need another plane."

CHAPTER 13

Louisiana

Cole poured another dollop of maple syrup on to his pancakes and bacon, then thrust a forkful into his mouth. Syrup dribbled over his chin and he wiped it with the back of his sleeve.

"Y'know, one good thing about England is the table manners," Aurora said. "Since when did people start eating breakfast in the afternoon, anyway?"

Cole grunted, and swigged his coffee. "You want those eggs?" he asked, pointing with his knife.

Aurora looked down at her own untouched plate. She'd called the Immortals earlier to warn them about Dr Fontaine, and learned about events at the Foundation. Since then she'd lost her appetite. Draka had escaped from the coin and ... Jonathan, dead. She'd thought Dodger was pulling her leg at first – some sort of sick joke – but she'd quickly understood he wasn't messing around. She'd never heard him sound like that – quiet, barely able to form words. She pushed the plate towards Cole. "Be my guest."

Cole grinned. "Full moon tonight. Got another sort of feast planned?"

Aurora shook her head. "I don't do that any more," she said. "Not unless I can find someone who really deserves it." She tapped her fingers on the table and looked around at the other clientele seated in the diner. Just a couple of truckers and a middle-aged couple who'd parked their motorhome in the lot outside. One old Latina woman in the kitchen, and a young waitress finishing her shift for the evening.

"You sure she's coming?" said Aurora. "Seems an odd place to—"

"She'll be here," said Cole, shovelling eggs into his face.

Aurora tried to relax, but she couldn't. Every moment she stayed here, the threat was growing. Draka was coming back to reclaim his body from the Blind Lagoon. The Immortals would be just behind. But really, did they have it in them? The price of stopping Draka last time had been great, and the pain seemed fresher than ever. She wasn't ready to lose any more friends.

Aurora pulled her hip flask out of her jacket and took a swig. Jonathan Harker had been a good man. Back in the early days, she'd never really liked Victor Frankenstein much – it was something about his eyes, always looking at her as if he half wanted to dissect her and learn the secrets of lycanthropy. It had been Harker who convinced her to join the Immortals. She'd always been told not to trust vampires, but Harker was different. He was a gentleman, and he knew what it was like to live with a curse. She couldn't imagine how Evelyn was feeling. Sure, the kid had been around for nearly two hundred years, but she was still too young to lose her pa.

"You know, I should warn you," said Cole. "She's changed."

"We've all changed," said Aurora. "It's been a long time."

Cole stirred more sugar into his coffee. "Hurricane Katrina hit her hard," he said. "She lost a grandchild. Even with her powers, she couldn't stop it."

The bell on the door tinkled. The girl behind the counter was wiping down a laminated menu but nodded as another woman in a shawl entered, carrying several grocery bags.

Aurora took another sip, wondering if she'd made an error coming here when she could have been at the Lagoon, setting an ambush. Dodger had said Luke had a theory that, while he'd been inside the coin, Draka had somehow fed off the spirits of the enemies defeated by the Immortals. Blue fire crackling from his hands, like Sanakhte. If that was true, he'd be more powerful than ever.

And the best way to fight magic was *with* magic.

Which is why Aurora had asked Cole to arrange the meeting.

"More coffee, sweetheart?" asked a new waitress. Aurora looked up to see a plump black woman holding a coffee pot. She did a double take.

"Marie?"

The witch's old wrinkled face hadn't changed at all, but Cole was right. Her eyes, once sharp and fearless, were deadened. For a second, though, they lit up, and a smile broke across her lips. Her toothless gums wore sparkling white dentures.

"Chile?" she said. "Is it really you?"

Aurora stood up and gave Marie Le Roux a hug. The witch's face came almost to her chest.

"Do you have a minute to talk?" asked Aurora, gesturing to the seat. Cole shifted along, taking his plate with him.

"I do for an ol' friend," said Marie, sitting down heavily. "My Lord, how long's it bin?"

"Too long," said Aurora. No more time to waste. "Listen, Marie, Draka is returning."

Marie's smile disappeared, and her face hardened. "You don't do small talk, do ya?"

Aurora explained briefly to her about Dr Fontaine and the possession, how Draka was at this moment flying over the Atlantic. She even shared Luke's theory that Draka had been growing stronger all the time he was trapped, and Marie looked grim.

While they were talking, one of the truckers was looking over. He clicked his fingers and gestured to his coffee cup, but Marie ignored him.

"He'll be searchin' for his body," she said.

"But you hid it, right?" said Aurora.

"I sure did, but that won't stop that devil. He'll sense its presence and stop at nothin' to find it."

"Hey!" said the trucker, banging a hand on the table. "What d'ya have to do to get a refill round here?"

"That's why we need your help," said Aurora.

Marie straightened and shook her head. "If that's why you're here, chile, you're gonna leave disappointed. Magic ain't my thing no more."

"Hey, lady!" said the trucker.

Aurora blocked him out, but she could feel her anger rising.

"You have to," she said.

The trucker stood up. "Don't make me come over there and get it myself."

"Want me to talk to him?" asked Cole.

Marie sighed, and wiggled her fingers. "What ya hollerin' for?" she snapped at the man. "You got a full cup right there'n front o' you."

The trucker frowned, and Aurora saw his cup was full

again. He didn't say thank you as he sat down, rubbing his head.

"That looked like magic to me," said Aurora.

"Of a piddlin' kind," said Marie. "If you're speakin' the truth about Draka, I ain't got the power to face him. Nor've you. Not on your own."

"I'll have the Immortals," said Aurora.

"And who might they be?" asked Marie.

"It's a long story," said Aurora.

"We got time," said Marie, nodded across the diner. The couple had left, so the place was pretty much empty.

So Aurora filled her in on her new friends – a vampire girl, a gargoyle, a street urchin with incredible speed, and finally Luke, a kid who'd died over a hundred and fifty years ago and been brought back to life with, amongst plenty of other enhancements, a reinforced skeleton, an external weapons dock on his forearm and an extendable electric sword.

"And you think they got it in them to fight Draka?" asked Marie.

"They'll fight," said Aurora, "and they'll give their lives if they have to. I'd rather it didn't come to that, though."

For a moment, she thought Marie was going to say "yes" – she could see thoughts crossing the old woman's wrinkled features. But then Marie stood up, brushed down her apron, and picked up the coffee pot. "I'm sorry, sweetheart. I can't help you."

"Why?" said Aurora.

"I ain't got it in me no more," said Marie, her face twisted with anguish. "I learned my limits the hard way."

She began to walk towards the counter and Cole shrugged. "Told you she weren't the same."

Aurora recalled what he'd said about the floods. She'd seen it in the news at the time – half the city swept away. Hundreds drowned. Hundreds of thousands left destitute. But no witch could have held back a deluge like that.

Aurora couldn't let Marie slip away. Had to convince her. Then she remembered Luke's words, and she knew a way.

"Draka said he'd feast on the city," she said. "He wants revenge on those who came after him. Back then, he took a few dozen. But New Orleans has grown."

Marie paused and lowered her head.

"This time he'll kill thousands," Aurora added. "The city needs you."

Marie turned around, spoke softly. "And if I let them down? Like I did before?"

"You won't," said Aurora. "We can do this. Together. You, me, Cole, the Immortals."

After a long pause, Marie nodded. "If Draka's as powerful as you say already, we'll need all the soldiers we can get. Gather the rest of the pack."

Aurora flashed a look at Cole. "I can't," she said. "Thane's the Alpha now. He won't allow—"

"Do it," said the witch. "That's the deal. I'll bring my magic, but you gotta bring your wolves."

"They're not mine to bring," said Aurora.

"Then change that," said Marie. "Become the Alpha." She placed a finger in the blinds and shifted them aside to look out at the dusk sky. "Moon will be up soon. Good night to settle old scores, I say. You know where to find me when it's done."

The old woman shuffled back behind the counter.

Aurora looked at Cole.

"I'm not going to like this plan, am I?" he said.

The Stein Foundation, Devon

"The plane's almost fuelled up," said Dodger, poking his head around the door of the busted-up lab.

Luke looked up from the array of needles and wires linked to a battery pack. "And I'm almost done here," he said.

Dodger squinted at the transferral apparatus, nonplussed. "You really think this will work?" he said.

"It has to," Luke replied.

Because it's the only hope Evelyn has. And the only way we might be able to stop Draka.

He had studied his father's experiment. It required a blood transfusion to be set up between Evelyn and the armour. Then an electric shock would cause the armour's powers of regeneration to flow into Evelyn, curing her of the BDS. And the armour would be stripped of its invulnerability. Two birds with one stone. That was the theory, anyway.

He placed the equipment into a cushioned case and slid that into his rucksack.

Making it had been the easy part, gathering transfusion wires and cannulas, and modifying a car battery to recreate a lightning strike. Finding the Blood Armour and carrying out the procedure would be the challenge.

Dr Pavlovic was waiting on the tarmac, wrapped in a warm coat and fur hat. It was ten at night, and Raziel stood at the top of the steps of a small sleek jet with ten windows on each side of the fuselage.

"Miss Harker is already on board," said Dr Pavlovic, as businesslike as ever. "We've cleared your flight plan with air traffic control, so you shouldn't have any bother from them. You have a higher top speed than Dr Fontaine – so with favourable weather conditions you should land not too far behind."

"Thank you," said Luke.

Slowly, she held out a hand. "I owe you a profound apology," she said more warmly. "I treated you with suspicion, when all the time our real enemy was lurking beneath my nose. I can't believe I brought him here."

Luke took the hand. "Fontaine took us all in," he said.

She gave a nod, eyes closed. "Good luck. When all this is over, we must speak properly, of the future."

If I'm still alive, thought Luke. He let go of her hand and bounded up the boarding steps in two strides. Raziel closed the door behind him, and turned the locking mechanism.

The plane was kitted out for luxury travel, with leather couches, mahogany furniture and stylish lamps. Normally, Luke would have been thrilled, but the sight of Evelyn lying on one of the sofas brought him to a halt. She looked terrible – gaunt and lifeless. The Blood Deprivation Syndrome was ravaging her much more quickly than it had affected Harker. But, above all, she looked terribly sad.

She smiled, though, as he walked up to her. "Oh, don't look like that," she said weakly. "I'm not dead yet."

"Just take it easy," said Luke. "It should only take us six hours or so. This jet is fast."

Evelyn doubled up, hands clutching at her middle with a groan of pain. Luke fell to his knees, arm around her shoulders. "What's the matter?"

Evelyn shuddered and gritted her teeth, but the attack passed. She looked at him through bloodshot, wild eyes. "What are you waiting for?" she said, suddenly serious. "Get us in the air."

Leaving his friend, Luke rushed to the front of the plane and climbed into the pilot seat beside Dodger.

"You can fly this thing, right?" said Dodger.

Luke strapped himself in. "Should be able to," he replied, trying to sound confident. The jet had ten times the amount of dials, knobs and switches as the chopper, but he closed his eyes and cleared his mind. *You can do this.* He had a basic piloting upload – it was just a case of accessing it. And one plane was much like another, surely? Differences of controls were just cosmetic.

He opened his eyes again, and let his brain take over. His hands started the jet turbines, and pushed the throttle. The plane's engines screamed.

"Er . . . brakes?" said Dodger.

Luke disengaged the wheel locks, and the plane jerked forward. Dodger cleared his throat and waved a sick bag. "Don't worry, guv, I've come prepared this time."

Luke eased the throttle forward more, using the rudder pedals to steer the plane in a slight curve towards the runway. Once they were parallel, he pressed the intercom. "Buckle up, everyone. Here we go."

He pushed the throttle firmly, locking it in auto-take-off position. He felt his body press back into the seat. The speed gauge rose to 50 mph, then 100, then 150. The rudder pedals became more sensitive as the airflow increased, and Luke pressed them gently to keep the accelerating plane in a straight line. *Wait for the right speed* . . . At 180 mph, Luke pulled back the yoke, and the aircraft's nose lifted above the horizon. With a mixture of relief and exhilaration, he felt the wheels leave the tarmac. Adrenaline flooded his veins as Dartmoor slid beneath them.

"Hey, we haven't died yet," said Dodger.

"Don't worry," said Luke. "There's plenty more danger where we're going."

"Like landing?" said Dodger with a grin.

Despite everything, Luke laughed as he set the autopilot for New Orleans airport.

Louisiana

Back on the road, this time with her heart thumping.

Aurora eased the throttle, accelerating the Harley along the potholed tarmac. It wasn't just the adrenaline coursing through her veins, though.

Just a few minutes until the moon appears. High noon for werewolves.

Aurora wasn't normally superstitious, but it being full moon seemed like fate. It was a cloudy evening, but it didn't matter. The wolf was undeniable. For years she'd learned to live with it, locking herself away rather than losing control to its appetites, but Harker had given her another way. The serum.

"There'll be more there tonight," said Cole over the growl of the bike engines. "Full moon, they all get together. Hunt as a pack."

"Good," said Aurora. "I don't want any doubters. I need them all to see."

Cole glanced across at her. They both knew what that meant. Thane wouldn't just relinquish pack leader status to her.

This fight will be to the death. Whose, time will tell.

She wondered when the plane carrying Draka would land. *Where* it would land. The Foundation had chartered another private jet from Plymouth, on the edge of Dartmoor. But at best they'd be an hour behind Draka. What would Marie make of them? It was true that, apart from Raziel, they didn't look like much. And if Evelyn had deteriorated, she might not be much use at all.

They pulled on to the dirt road towards the bar. Back into the wolves' den.

She slowed her bike to a stop.

"What's up?" said Cole, idling beside her.

Aurora reached into her jacket and took out a leather case. Inside was a syringe.

"Just a precaution," she said, rolling up her sleeve and inserting the needle into a blue vein in the crook of her elbow. She depressed the syringe and the contents flowed into her. "It lets the human part of my mind stay more in control when I transform. You want some?"

Cole grunted. "I've seen enough science today, thanks."

"You don't have to come, you know," she said. "You've

done enough already. This isn't your pack any more, remember."

"Don't get soppy on me, Cage," he replied. Then he grinned. "Anyway, I want to watch you kick Thane's ass."

Aurora twisted the throttle again. "I hope I don't disappoint."

Cole was right about the pack. There were about a dozen bikes parked up and several men and women sitting on the steps. Aurora recognised a couple from their scrap the night before. Injuries all healed, of course.

One man rushed straight inside as they pulled up twenty metres from the doors.

Aurora killed the engine and swung her leg over. The wolf was itching under her skin, ready to take over. Not long now.

Thane burst through the doors, knocking one of them off its hinges. Face already slick with sweat as the change came upon him.

"You shouldn't have come back, Cage," he said.

Aurora struggled to keep control. Her stomach felt knotted, but her mind stayed clear. The other werewolves came flooding out too.

"Draka's coming," she shouted, eyes sweeping across their faces. Some curious, some hostile. "I want to give you all a choice. Join me. Help me take care of him once and for all. If you don't, he'll become too strong. He won't care if it's humans or werewolves he slaughters. Your souls will belong to him."

"I gave you a chance," said Thane, his voice hoarse. "I won't give you another."

He nodded and the other members of the pack fanned out into a circle around them. A few were twitching and grimacing already. An animal scent in the air promised what was coming. Cole stayed at Aurora's side, but she shook her head. "My fight," she muttered.

"No way," he said.

"My fight!" she snapped, the last word more growl than human voice. Cole, back hunched like a dog with its tail between his legs, joined the others.

Aurora turned to Thane. "Let's settle this," she said. "Whoever wins leads the pack."

He walked slowly towards her, eyes glittering, then held out his hand. "You have my word."

As Aurora took it, Thane lurched forward, driving his forehead into the bridge of her nose. White light flared across her vision, followed by the inevitable pain. She managed to stay on her feet, and saw through tears that Thane was grinning. "When it's over," he said, "I'll let the rest of them eat your remains. Won't be nothin' left."

Aurora ran at him, anger rushing through her veins. She ploughed into his middle and they fell together on the floor. She heard the phone in her pocket crunch, and the crowd roared, pressing closer. Aurora saw the bloodlust in their faces as she punched Thane in the jaw with a left hook, then a right. He jerked his hips upward, and tossed her back over his head. She tried to stand and a kick caught her cheek and spun her around. Her teeth rattled on the steps to the bar, and she spat a mouthful of blood.

Thane cricked his neck. "This is easier than I thought," he said.

"Get him, Cage!" shouted Cole.

She feinted a punch to the face. Thane lifted an arm to block, and Aurora delivered a liver shot beneath his guard. He winced and crumpled up.

"Red Fur always said you were slow in the head," she said. She tried a kick, but he caught her foot and spun her around. She barrelled through the circle of spectators, and one stuck out a foot. She tripped, landed on her back. Thane pounced on to her in a flash.

She saw his massive hand swinging down, and he cuffed her across the ear with a brutal blow that left her head ringing. They rolled in the dirt, grappling, trying to pin each other. Thane's weight won out. He pushed her down and leaned in close, whispering in her ear.

"Slow, am I? Well, just so you know, I'm working with Fontaine. Have been for years."

Aurora strained. She couldn't believe what she was hearing. But Thane held her tight.

"How else do you think he got Beecher and the others?"

She felt rage bubble inside her. "Why?" Aurora croaked. She launched a wild punch to his ribs. Thane was ready. His hand darted forwards and gripped hold of her neck. He squeezed so tight she thought he might crush her windpipe. Damn, he was strong.

Thane grinned and Aurora realised he had wanted to make her angry, reckless. She grabbed his wrist and tried to pull his hand away, but he was pressing down on her with his entire bulk.

"I did it for the pack," said Thane. "A few pay the price so the rest can live."

"You're ... a fool," she croaked. Thane was pinning her with everything he had – and he was overbalancing. She drove a hand into his elbow joint, breaking his arm with a *snap*. Thane collapsed with a roar of pain, and she wriggled out from beneath him.

But she couldn't stand. And she saw why.

The moon was up.

The Alpha gripped his head and, one by one, the other men and women in the circle began to jerk and writhe.

Aurora tried to get to her feet again, but the pain was too great. She fell on to her back, not fighting it. Her bones strained towards breaking point and beyond, sinews cracking. Agony racked her – you never got used to it. Her skin felt aflame as bristles pushed through her pores. Her fingertips felt like they were dipped in acid as the claws broke out. Her muzzle stretched, dislocating her jaw, and her tongue licked over the sharp teeth sprouting from her gums. The air was alive with scents: agave, lint, woodsmoke, swamp water, tobacco, cleaning fluid, a thousand others she couldn't put a name to. Fear. She felt the urges of the wolf, but underneath it her thoughts were clear. She was glad for the serum in her veins. It was keeping her mind sharp. In control.

She looked across to the bar, where the other wolves rolled on the ground, some finding their paws already. Even the darkness was awash with colour through her wolf eyes. Thane was by far the biggest, his grey-black fur shaggy, one ear torn half away. His foreleg snapped back into place.

Aurora tipped back her head and the wolf voice emerged in a long howl aimed at the moon. The others joined, adding their mournful cries, reforming the circle around the two adversaries. Thane rose to face her, eyes a sickly yellow.

They both pounced together, meeting mid-air and tearing with their claws and teeth. Aurora sank her mouth into Thane's shoulder and shook him, tasting blood. But he somehow got his weight beneath her and tossed her over. She smashed into one of the werewolves spectating, barely turning around before Thane barrelled into her again. She landed on the steps of the bar, crunching through a set of wooden railings. He had a serious weight advantage. In a straightforward test of strength, she knew she couldn't win. The best weapon she had was her cunning.

As she stood, one of the other males to her left made a bite for her leg. In their wolf form, the rest of the pack were at the whim of their beast instincts, sensing a weak victim. She flashed her teeth and lunged, which drove him back. Thane was pacing, his mouth and claws bloody, in the centre of the circle.

Aurora picked herself up, pretending to be more badly injured than she was, tail between her legs. Thane darted at her, lashing out with a paw at her flank. She let his claws sink into her side, savouring the sharp focus of the pain, then gripped his leg in her front claws, pressing it further into her flesh. For a moment, realisation widened his eyes. He tried to pull free, but she had him pinned.

Aurora opened her jaws and snapped them closed around his throat. She felt the rush of his blood under her tongue and she shook her muzzle from side to side, then she tasted it too, pumping into her mouth. The taste of death.

Thane struggled, claws tearing at her, but his movements soon became weaker as the flow of his blood slackened. With a final shake, Aurora let his body sink to the ground.

She was panting hard, and badly injured too. But her wounds would heal by morning.

The other wolves watched her, then one by one they bowed their heads in supplication.

Aurora stood tall before them. She was the Alpha now, and no one could question it. There was only one thing left to do. A ritual in which she took no joy.

She gave the signal, and her pack set upon Thane's lifeless form.

CHAPTER 14

The flight had taken five hours so far. Dodger slept for four and three-quarter hours of it. Every time Luke glanced at him, his co-pilot's headphones were sitting more awry across his stove-pipe hat. Dr Pavlovic was true to her word – they didn't get so much as a query from air traffic control. It was dark the whole way, as they followed the night-time through several time zones. Beneath them was darkness, too – the formless and mighty Atlantic. Luke couldn't help but think of his father making this journey as a young man – he had often spoken of the gale-swept seas when Luke was just a boy on his knee. It had taken him two months by boat.

And what would my dad think of me now? Luke wondered.

He managed a grim smile as he imagined what his father would make of the modern apparatus in his satchel, recreating his most secret of experiments. *He'd be impressed.*

The first proper land they sighted was the Florida Keys, the string of islands sitting in shallow azure seas. Luke guided the plane as the instruments told him, skirting north of the Caribbean and looping over the Gulf of Mexico.

From above, New Orleans spread like a glittering tapestry, surrounded by a million dark channels of bayou, as the sea encroached like the fronds of a plant into the reclaimed land around the city.

"Ever seen anything like it?" muttered Dodger.

"Never," said Luke. The furthest he'd ever travelled was Athens, on a family holiday when he was eight. For the first time it occurred to Luke how far away he was from home.

"We're not in Bethnal Green any more," Dodger muttered.

He steered a path away from the city itself, at which point the instruments let out a series of pings.

Dodger stirred. "You're going the wrong way, mate," he said.

"No, I'm not," said Luke.

Luke had known all along that landing in the New Orleans main airport wasn't an option. Draka wouldn't brook any delay in reaching his body – he'd go there by the fastest possible route. Luke would have to do the same. He'd already found the coordinates of the Blind Lagoon and inputted them into the plane's navigation system. It was situated several miles outside the city, and they'd just have to ditch the plane as near as possible.

He explained all this to Dodger, who looked at him as if he was mad.

"But what if there's no airfield?" he asked.

"We'll find a road," said Luke, taking the plane to lower altitude.

"A road?" said Dodger. "Sorry, Luke me boy, I'd trust you with my life and all, but perhaps this piloting upload's made your noggin soft. You can't land a plane on a road."

"Why not?" asked Luke.

"Because ..." said Dodger, waving his arms. "Because ..."

Luke eased down the air speed and they sank further through a clear sky, a contrast of fields, settlements and mangroves growing larger. He had no idea if it would work, but what other choice was there? They were sixty miles from the Lagoon, and at their current speed they'd cover that distance in a matter of minutes.

Raziel entered the cockpit, bending low. He was holding Evelyn in his arms. She lay semi-conscious, a sheen of sweat over her brow.

Luke's chest tightened at the sight of his friend, usually so strong, lying limp and vulnerable in the huge stone arms. "How is she?" he asked.

"Worse all the time," said Raziel quietly. "She mumbles

in her sleep, but I cannot make out the words, other than 'father'."

"We'll be landing soon," Luke said. "It might be a little ... bumpy. Take care of her."

Raziel nodded gravely.

Luke's heart felt empty. He wondered how long his friend had left.

Several alarms across the console brought his attention back to the landing. They were cruising at a thousand feet, and the plane's controls were asking Luke to confirm that he wanted to fly below that ceiling.

"Even the plane doesn't think this is a good idea," said Dodger.

"There!" said Luke. He pointed to a long stretch of freeway below, a straight grey strip with no habitations in sight. It was dark, but thankfully the full moon offered some illumination. There was no sign of Draka's plane. That gave Luke a glimmer of hope. If they could get there first, they had a chance of stopping Draka from even reaching his body.

"Looks sort of narrow, doncha think?" asked Dodger.

Luke lined up the plane, and reduced speed. Dodger groaned.

Trees lined one side of the road, lagoon the other.

If I get this wrong, it'll be a fiery grave. Or a watery one.

Luke activated the landing gear and held the wheel steady, trying not to grip too tight.

"Just pretend it's a simulation," he muttered under his breath.

"Er ... no, pretend it's real!" said Dodger. "Pretend the life of your very dear friend the Artful Dodger is reliant on landing this plane safely!"

Luke blocked him out and focused on the road. Airspeed was down to 150 and dropping. It felt good. "A few seconds until touchdown." The road approached. It was narrow, but there was enough clearance for the wings either side. The altimeter was beeping calmly, telling him the descent was safe. Luke lifted the nose a fraction. Then he brought down the landing gear, ready to set the aircraft down.

"Hell's bells!" screamed Dodger. "Look out!"

Two headlights coming right at them – a huge truck. Luke drove the throttle forward for extra speed and the plane rose sharply. Luke saw the trucker's eyes like saucers for a split second, and then they were clear.

Luke's heart was trying to leap out of his chest but he gathered himself and pushed the yoke down again, dipping the aircraft. The rear wheels bounced and skidded on the road surface, then the nose wheels touched too. Luke eased in the brakes, eyes peeled for any other traffic. Not that he knew what he'd do if anything headed their way.

The plane dropped to a safe speed, bumping along the road. Luke noticed what looked like a logger's yard off to one side. Eventually the plane came to a halt, and Luke killed the engine. His breaths came fast, and he realised his hands were shaking. He hardly believed they'd made it.

A grin flashed on Dodger's bloodless face. "Welcome to Louisiana," he said.

Under the full moon, Dodger tugged the airboat's ignition wire for the third time, and nothing happened.

"No joy, guv," he said. "I think it's dead."

"Let me try," said Luke, walking across the back of the boat. He took the toggle and pulled himself. The motor growled into life and the giant fan began to spin idly.

"Yeah, well, you've got an unfair advantage," said Dodger. "We ain't all got enhanced strength."

Luke felt the airboat thrum beneath his feet. Evelyn wobbled and he steadied her, supporting her weight as she sat down.

She looked terrible, like a moving corpse. But she had at least regained consciousness, insisting she could walk herself. She'd taken a few stumbling steps from the aircraft, before tripping and falling. Raziel had had to carry her as they jogged off the highway towards the Blind Lagoon.

Their onward journey would be by water.

Finding the boathouse was a stroke of luck. A hefty padlock was all the security they'd come across, and Dodger made short work of that.

"You take to the air," said Luke to Raziel, after he lowered

Evelyn into the boat's seat. The boat rocked as the gargoyle stepped back on to the jetty beside the beaten-up shack, and took off with heavy wingbeats.

Luke dropped his satchel into the airboat, careful not to damage any of the precious equipment inside. Then he drove the throttle forward. The fan spun to a blur and the flat-bottomed craft moved out of the boathouse into open water. The dark surface rippled, creating curves of white where the moon's rays landed. The mangrove trees rose like strange organic columns from their thick bases, reflected in the water. There wasn't another human soul out here, but Luke's ears picked up eerie animal calls drifting through the dense foliage. Though there was no map, Luke's internal GPS flashed the coordinates Aurora had given them. It was about a mile away. The cave that held the Blood Armour.

He wondered what they'd find there. They'd spoken to Aurora before leaving, and she'd mentioned traps. But Luke was hopeful. *As long as Draka hasn't got there first.*

Luke wondered how Aurora was getting on. She had said she was fetching help. He hoped she would catch up with them soon. But now the full moon was up, Luke knew she would be in her wolf form, and out of contact.

"You got a face like a sunken pudding," said Dodger.

"I'm just worried about Aurora," Luke replied.

Dodger nodded. "She'll be all right, y'know."

"I hope so," said Luke, "because we need her."

Their boat cut a wake through the still water as they threaded their way between banks of land. Alligators appeared in Luke's night vision, resting in the shallows, just breaching the surface, but they didn't seem interested in Luke and his companions. He looked up and saw Raziel flying low over the trees like some sort of prehistoric creature. Luke couldn't help fearing the worst. Without Aurora, could the four of them really take on Draka? He shot a glance at Evelyn, who was slumped in the driver's chair.

Make that three of us.

The waterway narrowed as the trees closed in on either side. Luke slowed the fan. According to his GPS, they were closing on the caves, but spits of land blocked their path. Luke steered perpendicular to their destination, looking for a channel through, as the boat parted the lily pads covering the waterway like a dark green carpet. The bird sounds, Luke noticed, had ceased, and a slightly rotten scent hung on the air. Evelyn coughed in the back, a racking sound that seemed to grip her whole body. Her eyelids were fluttering.

This is taking too long, thought Luke. *This place is a labyrinth.*

Luke shuddered at the thought that Draka had reached the cave already. If he had managed to get to the Blood Armour, the procedure to transfer its power to Evelyn would be impossible. His friend would be beyond help and Draka back to full power.

"Dodger, take the tiller," he said.

Luke waved up to Raziel, and gestured him to fly down. "I'm going to look with Raziel from the air," he said. "The cave is close, but with all this vegetation we'll never see it."

Raziel swooped low, and landed on the side of the airboat, making it tip precariously in the water. "Can you give me a lift?" Luke asked.

Raziel nodded, so he scrambled on to the gargoyle's broad back. Luke marvelled at how the stone could be so hard, yet also flexible. He gripped Raziel's neck as they took off. In a matter of seconds they were above the trees.

"Let's find this cave," said Luke.

The bayou stretched for miles in every direction, without any human habitation, but there was a solid mass of ground towards the north, about a hundred metres away. Luke let the cool breeze caress his face as he guided Raziel by pressing lightly on one shoulder. They wheeled towards it and Luke squeezed his knees against the gargoyle's warm flanks. According to his GPS, they were right on top of it.

Luke spotted a patch of raised ground to his right. "Looks a good bet for a cave," said Luke.

"Indeed," replied the gargoyle.

As they flew closer, there was no sign of Draka or any other boat.

"Let's get the others," he said.

Raziel turned back towards the airboat, flying low over the water, following the maze of channels between the mangroves. Luke memorised the route and, as Raziel slowed by banking his wings, Luke dropped down on to the vessel, making it rock.

"Meet us there," Luke called to the gargoyle. "We've found it," he said to Dodger, taking the tiller. "Hold on, Evelyn."

She didn't reply, but a weak smile spread across her lips.

Luke drove the boat onward, determination hardening in his heart. If they'd somehow managed to get here first . . .

The water exploded, and Evelyn screamed.

Luke twisted around to see a beast leaping up in a fountain of spray. His eyes registered a long, scaly head, and water dripping from rows of dagger teeth, and his brain processed it a split second later. *Alligator!*

Dodger leapt back as the tail thrashed the water to froth and the creature scrambled further into the boat, reaching for Evelyn with single-minded hunger.

CHAPTER 15

Something was wrong with the alligator's eyes, but Luke's lightning blade was out before he could tell what it was. He slashed at the creature's tough scales. He wasn't sure if he had injured it or not, but it snarled and withdrew.

"Get us out of here, Dodger!" he yelled.

There were more alligators now, pressing from each side. Their eyes were completely red, he realised, as if covered in blood, but they seemed to know exactly where they were going. Another reared its upper half from the water, but Raziel swept down and gripped it in his fists, rising upwards with the writhing creature. He dropped it like a stone into the mangroves.

Dodger pushed the throttle to max and Luke almost lost his footing as the boat roared forward. The prow thumped into alligators blocking the way, each one slowing the craft.

Luke knew enough to realise this wasn't natural behaviour – they were being controlled.

Draka was already here.

One of the creatures smashed its tail into the fan housing, and the boat swerved. Evelyn crashed into Luke and they almost rolled over the side. The engines stalled, leaving the boat dead in the water. The alligators churned the surface, closing in.

"We're surrounded," said Dodger, opening his jacket and fishing among all the vials and grenades hanging inside.

Luke reached over the side and stabbed at an alligator, but then drew back sharply as another snapped for his arm.

Fear seemed to have given Evelyn a jolt. She was tugging ineffectually on the ignition again, trying to get the fan started. Alligators buffeted the boat from all sides. One sank its teeth into the fibreglass hull, biting off a chunk. Water shipped over the edge. Evelyn yanked again, then her knees gave way in exhaustion.

Luke grabbed the cord in her place. "Dodger, can't you do something?" he said.

"Give us a minute," said Dodger. "Ah – this should do the trick." He took out a small globe. "Hold on to your hats." He tossed it among the reptiles.

"I'm not wearing a—" said Luke.

BOOM! The whole boat rose and the water turned white

as something detonated in the depths. Stunned alligators surfaced, rolling in panic. Luke pulled on the cord desperately and the engine came to life. The prow lifted and he steered a path through the gators, heading straight towards dry land.

"We're going to crash," said Evelyn. Her hair hung down over her face.

"That's the idea," said Luke. As they reached the northern shore, he angled the prow towards a shallow bit of the bank. The boat bounced up, beaching on the mud. He killed the engine. Throwing his satchel over his shoulder, he took one of Evelyn's arms, while Dodger took the other. They clambered out of the airboat on to the shore. The alligators slowed as they approached, drifting to a stop, and remained in the water, staring with their red gaze.

"Look at them mince pies," said Dodger.

"What?" said Evelyn. She felt to Luke like nothing more than skin and bones under her clothes.

"He means 'eyes'," he said. "Don't you remember what Aurora said? Draka can control the minds of other predators." *But why aren't they still attacking?*

One by one, the alligators sank out of sight.

"Well, come on," said Dodger. "Let's scram before they decide they're still hungry."

Raziel landed too, his feet squelching as he set them down on the bank and closed his wings.

"There's another boat," he said. "Further up the shore. I cannot tell if it has been used recently."

Luke's skin prickled. *What if we're too late?*

They set off, back towards where he'd spotted the mound. The ground was soft underfoot, littered with snaking roots. With all the mangrove trunks, it was hard to see far ahead. Luke kept an eye out for any sign of ambush, but apart from the shadows of the swaying branches, cast by the full moon, nothing stirred.

"Remember what Aurora said," Luke whispered. "The cave might be booby-trapped." The mention of Aurora made Luke wish once more that she would catch up with them soon.

Dodger hitched Evelyn's arm up higher over his shoulder. "So Draka might not make it through anyway," said Dodger hopefully.

Luke wasn't hopeful. He quickened his steps, and kept his lightning blade extended. Evelyn hung off his free arm. If it came to a pitched battle, he knew she had no strength to fight.

"Just focus on the Blood Armour," she said, as though reading his thoughts. "I'll look after myself."

They passed into an area where the trees seemed to be half-decomposed, the branches bare, and they formed a ring around a clearing. Luke saw he was right about the cave. Its entrance was only one and half metres high, but twice as wide, with vines trailing over the mouth.

"That must be it," said Dodger. His eyes swept the ground. "Can't see any footprints. Looks like we beat old baldy."

Luke wasn't so sure. He sensed, with a tickle up and down his spine, that they were being watched.

Then the ground on the edges of the clearing came alive. Luke jumped. A tide of alligators slithered into view. Twenty of them at least. All with the same blood-red gaze.

"Not these lot again," said Dodger. "Hold her for a sec, would you?" Luke took Evelyn's weight as Dodger reached into his jacket. He cracked the top of a vial and tossed in into the trees. Blue smoke cascaded down on to a group of the reptiles, scattering them. Some sort of hydrochloric acid, Luke guessed.

But, as the smoke cleared, the reptiles regrouped, then scurried forward, blocking off the cave mouth.

With a sweep of his wings, Raziel launched through the air. He thumped down on to two more of the beasts. They squirmed under his talons, but the rest came straight for Evelyn. Luke let her down, and she slumped to the earth. Then he stood in front of her. The cave was agonisingly close, just past the snapping line of reptiles.

"You go," Raziel called, as if reading his thoughts. "We will protect her." The gargoyle sprang to Luke's side, spreading his stone wings like a barrier.

"I guess so," added Dodger. He threw a metal star at the ground in front of an approaching reptile, making it back off. "We'll follow in a bit."

"I don't need protecting," Evelyn muttered, flicking open her staff, and pushing herself unsteadily upright. "Go get him, Luke."

"I'm not leaving you," said Luke. One alligator darted for Evelyn's leg, and Luke ducked and swivelled, driving his searing hot lightning blade into its mouth. It rolled in a frenzy, smoke trailing from its mouth, before falling in a heap. But more approached.

"Then we all die," said Evelyn. "Please, Luke – I don't have long."

He stared at her pleading face. *She's right. This is our only hope.* He could stay and fight, but Evelyn would die without the Blood Armour. And if Draka got to it before him, an unimaginable number of innocent lives would be lost too in the wake of the Soul Hunter.

The mass of alligators shuffled to a stop around the Immortals, their muscular bodies tense and ready to strike. Leaving his friends at their mercy felt wrong . . . "Stop dilly-dallyin'," shouted Dodger.

The alligators attacked. Raziel flew into a group of them, beating them back from Evelyn. Dodger darted in front of the vampire girl, potions exploding around him and his dagger a flash of steel. "Go, lad!" he shouted at Luke.

Luke took a breath, drew his lightning blade, and sprinted into the tide of scales and teeth, the equipment inside his satchel rattling. Luke raised his lightning blade, but, surprisingly, the alligators backed off, their crimson eyes gazing at him warily. *Maybe they're scared of the lightning blade*, Luke thought as he dodged between them. He jumped over the last group of three-metre monsters, then reached the cave, plunging into the darkness. He could hear the sounds of battle behind him, but forced himself to ignore them.

The lightning blade offered little illumination. Even with his enhanced night vision, he could only see about twenty metres ahead. Bare rock walls, covered in lichen and moss. Hard-packed earth underfoot. Rocks and boulders scattered in a few places. An eerie atmosphere hung inside the cave, and Luke felt a tingle down his neck. He felt like he was being observed. A flicker of movement in the shadows made him swivel. A bat flapped out and flew off in the direction of the entrance.

The sounds of snarling and battle cries from outside quickly faded as he edged further down the passageway. He tried to forget about his companions and focus ahead. He knew there were going to be traps. His heart was knocking in his chest, his breathing heavy. He quickened his steps, turning on the heat vision on his ocular lens. If anything was lurking in wait he didn't want to be caught off guard.

The trail descended steeply. After skidding a few times, he steadied himself against the cold, damp wall. Luke fought the claustrophobia, ignoring the close stifling atmosphere, loaded with danger. Every sense told him to turn back, but he pushed onward.

The ground ahead looked black, and then his stomach lurched. Not ground at all, but a sheer drop.

It was less than two metres to the other side. Even in Dr Fontaine's body, Draka would have no problem at all, and neither would Luke. He took a step back, clasped the satchel close to his side, then ran at the gap.

But something brought him skidding to a halt. "It's too easy," he muttered to himself.

Two metres? Maybe not even that. Anyone – even a child – could make it across.

What if it's a trick?

Luke stooped and picked up a small pebble. Gently, he tossed it across the abyss.

Halfway, the pebble stopped in the air as it impacted with some invisible barrier. Briefly, a green wall of light flashed, spanning the tunnel in mid-air. With its path blocked, the pebble plummeted. Luke didn't hear it land.

He sucked in a deep breath. *That could have been me. I need to be more careful.*

But how could he get across? The force field had vanished again, but Luke thought he'd noticed something when it had blinked into existence. He took another stone and repeated the throw. This time he watched the top of the wall instead of the stone, and saw that, as he'd suspected, it didn't reach right to the roof of the cavern. There was a gap. Only a metre, but big enough for him to pass.

The problem was – how to get up there?

Luke opened his satchel and took out the grapple-gun attachment, locking it on to the inserts in his metal arm, feeling the mechanism connect to his nerve endings, where it could be controlled with one thought. He set it for *penetration* and the hook flipped out to form a long point with barbs behind. He aimed at the cavern roof. It would make a hell of a noise, but there was no point in hiding now. He pulled the trigger and the metal head thumped into the rock, showering splinters. Luke tugged on the other end, making sure the barbs were in place. Then leaned all his weight on it. It held.

Now for the scary part.

Gripping the grapple-gun tightly, he stepped off the ledge, and let the high-tensile alloy wire support him, as he swung across and banged into the force field. For a moment, he hung there, expecting the thing to give way and the blackness to swallow him up. When it didn't, he activated the winch setting, and let the gun's electric winch lift him to the top of the shimmering wall. He clambered over the top, so he was sitting astride it, then disengaged the grapple. Luke jumped the three-foot gap to the other side easily, landing in a crouch.

One down ... How many more to go?

He was about to keep moving, when he had a final thought. He pulled off his jacket and tossed it over the top of the wall. As soon the fabric touched the magical barrier, it blinked into life and stayed lit up. If the others followed, they'd see the trap for what it was.

The force field also threw some light on the way ahead. The tunnel turned a corner. The air seemed cooler down here. *I can do this.* If he kept his head—

Luke dived forwards as someone attacked from the right. He came up in a defensive posture, his lightning blade ready. But it wasn't a person – it was a swinging pendulum of heavy timber with a blade at the end, scything back and forth from a hidden alcove.

"So much for keeping my head," he mumbled. *I nearly lost it then.*

He scanned the ground but couldn't see any tripwire that had set the trap off. It must have been triggered magically. He didn't want to move, in case another appeared from nowhere. He tried to think of a way to let the others know, but couldn't come up with anything. Unless ...

He grabbed one of the sticky grenades from his satchel. They were designed to incapacitate an enemy by coating them in a heavily adhesive compound. Perhaps he could use it on the pendulum mechanism. He tossed the grenade at the hinge where the top of the swinging blade connected with the roof of the tunnel. It exploded with a dull splat, and almost at once the pendulum began to slow, creaking to a halt after a few seconds.

Two traps passed. Still alive ...

Luke trod carefully, ready to dive if another blade appeared. But none did, and after another twenty paces or so, he reached a wooden door. It had probably been untouched for almost two centuries, but you couldn't tell. Like the pendulum, there was no sign of rotting, or mould. Luke wondered if it was magic that had preserved the traps. He stepped closer and inspected the door. Wood couldn't carry a current, so electrocution was out of the question, but there was no saying how else it could be rigged to kill him. He stood back and tossed another stone from a metre away. It bounced off harmlessly.

Sometimes a door is just a door ...

Luke edged forward, and kicked out. The door swung open with a low creak.

On the other side was another passageway, wider, and dimly lit from a source of light he couldn't make out. And still no sign of the Blood Armour. He crept through.

It slammed closed at his back, and all the lights vanished.

Luke inhaled a rush of panicked breath as he spun in the pitch-blackness and tried to find the handle. There wasn't one. He tried to smash the door with his shoulder, but it felt solid. So he turned again. His UV and infrared picked up nothing. And for some reason, as he looked down, even his lightning blade was invisible. He tried to control the rising wave of panic.

This isn't normal darkness. Something – some magic – was preventing him seeing as part of the test.

He shuffled on, then heard a swishing sound. He ducked, and felt something swing past his head, just millimetres away. It swung back again.

Another pendulum.

Fear gripped his heart like a fist as more sounds reached his ears. Soft hisses, and whistles, and breaths of air. He didn't need his eyes to know the room had come alive with mechanical traps. Blades and bludgeons waiting for him in the blackness, each one deadly.

He rallied against the rising terror, calming his pulse, trying to make himself think clearly. He couldn't let Evelyn down. There was only one way to go – onward. Even if it meant almost certain death.

Trust your instincts, said a voice in his head.

Harker had spoken those words, in the early hours after Luke's reanimation. He'd explained that Luke's brain was capable of amazing things, but it couldn't be forced. He had to let his heightened senses work freely, without conscious effort.

Luke stayed in a crouch, closing his useless eyes and letting his ears take over. Letting his skin feel the currents of air disturbed by the swinging weapons. Sure enough, the shape of the passage began to appear in his mind's eye – a shape made up of sounds and sensations rather than visual perception. Luke allowed the rhythms of the death chamber to guide him as he hurried forward, swaying back occasionally, or darting forwards to let a heavy object sweep by. He sensed another and sidestepped, letting it whistle past. Then he jumped as something swung at his legs, and rolled beneath a blade.

But as he tried to stand, his satchel strap snagged on something and he lost his balance. His senses fell into chaos, and he suddenly didn't know which way to go. He felt something hit his hip, spinning him round. He collided with another moving object, and staggered. The terror returned, flaring across his chest, and then a breath of wind flickered his fringe.

He realised something was coming for his head.

He didn't have time to dodge, and lifted his arm to block it.

A flash of agony, then weightlessness as the force lifted him off his feet and through the air. He slammed into wood, which splintered and gave way under his weight.

Luke landed on the other side, and saw he'd broken through a door. Light spilled over the pendulums as they chopped and slashed in a dizzying array of blades and clubs and spikes. The nearest one had shattered into fragments of wood. He'd made it through, but his arm felt all wrong. The skin was split open in a huge gash. His hand hung limply, and the metal implant beneath his forearm gleamed with blood. It was slightly dented, and the lightning blade within shone dully. He tried to summon it, but it simply juddered in its housing. It looked like the alloy joints of his wrist had twisted out of shape, blocking the blade. He willed it out harder, and managed to extend it slightly, but the bent casing caused it to push against his flesh, sizzling. Luke cried out from the pain.

His satchel lay on the floor, and he scrambled beneath the smashed pendulum and tugged it towards him. If any of the crucial apparatus inside were damaged, this would all have been for nothing.

Luke sagged in relief when he saw the battery and transfusion wires were intact. His body felt broken, but he knew he didn't have time to recuperate. He clenched his eyes closed at the terrible thought that Evelyn might be dead already. *Don't think like that.*

"Keep going," he urged himself. Luke looped the satchel back over his shoulder, and returned to the broken door. In the chamber on the other side were two chests, made of a white stone that shone with minute embedded crystals. One was long and coffin-shaped. The Blood Armour, surely. Cobwebs stretched across the room and the chests, and the floor was covered in sand. Nothing looked remotely disturbed.

Luke grinned, despite the pain in his arm. He'd got here first, which meant Draka hadn't made it. Now all they had to do was bring Evelyn through, and hook her up to the Blood Armour. He unhooked his rucksack with the equipment and took a step towards the chests, eager to see what they contained.

When he heard the shuffle of steps behind him, he didn't have time to turn before something struck the back of his head.

The room spun, and sand lurched up to meet him.

CHAPTER 16

When Luke opened his eyes the figure of Fontaine was standing over him, blood-red eyes glaring madly against the black backdrop of the cavern ceiling.

"You truly are a fine specimen," the man said in Draka's guttural voice, "and your spirit will taste sweet to my parched throat."

Luke's mind fought through waves of nausea and pain. He wanted to stand, but his limbs wouldn't obey. Draka lifted a foot and stamped on his chest, forcing Luke back into the sand. He felt so stupid as he realised what must have happened.

Draka was following me the whole time! Luke remembered how the alligators had backed away from Luke, then the creeping feeling of being watched, inside the cave. *Draka wanted me to enter. He was here already, watching.*

Luke had successfully passed all the tests, and in doing so he had led their enemy to the chamber where his body was hidden, the key to restoring his full power.

The Soul Hunter himself was staring at the chests, enrapt.

Luke wondered if there was any chance Dr Fontaine himself still had some control? If so, could he reach that human part within?

"You don't have to do this," he said. "You're a scientist. You help people. This isn't the cure you're looking for."

The red eyes bore into Luke. "You waste your breath," he said. "The man's soul is mine already."

Then they both heard a thump and Draka looked to the chests. Luke turned his head too and saw the lid of one had shifted a fraction.

"Come to me!" said Draka's voice. "Let us join spirit and flesh once more and take our revenge on the cursed city!"

Another thump and the lid rocked off the top, crashing on to the floor.

The red eyes died and the face of Fontaine gasped. Luke realised the scientist was back in control of his body for the moment, seeing through his own eyes again. His face was racked with pain. He began to spasm from head to foot, as if some powerful force was shaking his body. Luke managed to push himself away as the scientist's body rose off the floor, arms and legs splayed out. He opened his mouth and

Luke expected a scream, but instead a bright red light burst from his lips. Then his eyes seemed to explode into dazzling rays as well. Luke smelled burning flesh. Fontaine's face was crackling. He began to groan horribly as the lights snaked from his body towards the open chest. The spirit of Draka was leaving the scientist and streaming towards the Blood Armour.

Luke looked on in horror. *If they join again, we're all doomed.*

Like a light bulb shorting, the lights died and Dr Fontaine's body dropped to the floor in a heap. He was steaming slightly, his skin burned black in places. There was no way he could have survived.

Luke rolled to his side and on to all fours. He stared at the chest, unable to rip his gaze away.

Something rose from within.

A human shape, but much bigger, with a huge upper body rippling with muscle. Every inch of skin was dark red like coagulated blood. The bald head was a block of gleaming flesh, with a wide mouth and narrow-spaced eyeballs staring from beneath a Neanderthal brow, and open holes for ears and nose. Skinless, the features were just stretched sinew and tendons.

Draka was in the Blood Armour.

He heaved a deep breath as he clambered out from the stone coffin. He wore only a loincloth, and his legs were trunks of muscle. His massive arms seemed too long for his body, almost gorilla-like, ending in spade-like hands.

The Soul Hunter looked upon Luke for a moment, then grunted and walked to the second chest. As if it weighed nothing at all, he lifted the stone lid and tossed it aside, smashing it to pieces on the wall. He reached inside.

Luke looked over Fontaine's corpse towards the door. Every fibre of his being wanted to run for safety – to put as much distance between Draka and himself as possible – but then he spotted his satchel near the entrance.

Evelyn's life depends on me. Even if I can weaken him, it might give us a chance to carry out the procedure.

Luke watched as Draka picked out a breastplate of thick, scaly armour and placed it over his head.

Alligator skin...

He attached other pieces to his legs and forearms. Luke looked at his lightning blade, trapped in his arm. Even if he could summon it, he wondered what harm he could possibly cause to Draka.

I might as well try to bring down a rhino with a butter knife.

Next, the towering red demon retrieved a quiver of arrows, each at least a metre long, and a bow twice as tall as Luke and made of gleaming white bone. Draka looped both over his shoulders as if he had all the time in the world.

Luke tried to summon his lightning blade again, and this time it edged further out, every millimetre burning his flesh. He bit his tongue to stop himself from crying out.

Draka bowed over the chest. Luke realised he might not get another chance. He scrambled up and charged, leaping over the broken lid and throwing himself at the demon.

The Soul Hunter swatted with an arm, and the blow hurled Luke across the chamber. He slammed into a wall and collapsed in a crumpled heap at the base.

Draka let his red gaze rest on Luke.

"I watched you, boy," he said, and his voice boomed across the chamber. "All those years when I was imprisoned, I watched and fed off the spirits of those you vanquished. Their dying cries were nectar to me, nourishing me in my dark hours. Your own pain will be sweeter still."

Luke managed to stand, but his legs felt wobbly. "Yeah, well, good luck with that."

Draka placed a necklace over his head, threaded with rattling skulls. One was clearly an alligator's, and another had once belonged to a werewolf, Luke guessed. The third looked like a big cat of some sort, and the last a human's, cracked along the scalp. "I will strip the flesh from your skull and honour you among my victims," said the Soul Hunter.

"No thanks," said Luke.

He scanned Draka's armour, searching for the best area to strike. If indeed he managed to land a blow at all.

"I sense your doubts, boy," said Draka. "You are right to be afraid. I have grown so powerful in my long confinement."

"Love the sound of your own voice, don't you?" said Luke.

Draka's brows knitted in a scowl and he shot a beam of blue energy from his hands. Luke felt it slam into his chest, then grip him like a vice and hoist him into the air. He couldn't move at all as the beam dragged him towards Draka. He fought the urge to cry out in pain as his bones ground against one another. Draka watched him all the way, then closed a hand over Luke's throat as the energy died.

Luke couldn't breathe at all in the demon's grip.

"The pharaoh's magic is strong," said Draka, a smile on his lipless mouth. He sighed. "But I had hoped you would offer me a fight."

"Try this," Luke croaked. With all his effort, he forced the lightning blade to extend through the remnants of his lower wrist, and jammed it into the Soul Hunter's bicep.

Draka tipped back his head and roared with anger as the blade's current passed through his body. He dropped Luke like a sack of potatoes. Luke scrambled away, clawing at the sand, his body numb and racked with pain from the magical energy. *At close quarters, I don't stand a chance.*

Draka kicked out in rage, and Luke rolled away. The demon's foot smashed the stone chest which had held his armour into pieces. The Soul Hunter flailed in pain, gripping his injured arm. He slammed into the doorway, shaking the whole chamber. Rocks began to fall from the ceiling, bouncing off his armour-clad back. Smaller fragments cascaded over Luke.

Draka paused as the crumbling ceased. Luke saw the cut to the Soul Hunter's arm was already healing, the red skin restoring itself. But Draka remained by the door, looking up at the chamber's roof.

He's scared, thought Luke. *Scared of being trapped again.*

Luke stood up, dust showering from his clothes, then pointed his bladed arm at Draka. "What are you waiting for?" he said. "Fight me."

The Soul Hunter smiled. "Perhaps I underestimated you, Luke Frankenstein. But there will be time for that. The age of Draka is here at last, and it will last for an eternity. I will begin with your friends, savouring their deaths, and then the city that once tried to destroy me. If you still live when all that is done, we will meet again."

"Come on, then!" said Luke.

"Patience," said Draka. "Your death will come when I hunger for it the most. I will savour your unique essence – the hero born of science. For now, this place will be your prison."

As Luke ran at him again, Draka drove a fist into the wall, and the chamber trembled. Luke stumbled back to avoid a falling boulder slamming in front of him. Another glanced off his shoulder, knocking him to his knees. The last thing he saw was Draka slipping away into darkness, before the whole cavern collapsed around him in a thunder of stone.

CHAPTER 17

A crushing weight on his chest. Dark, but not pitch-black. He'd lost consciousness, but for how long? Luke saw chinks of light through the rocks above. His lungs begged for a deep breath, but he couldn't take one. His mouth was gritty, and he spat out a gobbet of dust-filled saliva. *Don't panic.* He tried to move his toes. *I can feel them. That's good.* But his arms were trapped. He could wiggle his fingers, but barely shift his arms. He strained against the rocks. Nothing moved.

Buried alive.

The words rose up unbidden, and with them came fear and a rush of claustrophobia that made him break out in a sweat all over his body. He wanted to call for help. But what good would it do? He guessed was over fifty metres underground.

And Draka was heading straight for the others.

Luke gritted his teeth and pushed again. Rocks dug into his arms and legs. He pushed and pushed, then fell back, panting. Fought off the terror.

What would it mean, if he couldn't get free? He was immortal. He couldn't die; he had to be killed. If no one came to kill him, how long would he lie down here, in the cold and dark? Until he went mad, or tried to bash out his own brains against the rocks? No, Draka would return, he'd promised. He'd come back for Luke, full of the souls of the other Immortals and all the city of New Orleans.

Luke couldn't let that happen.

"No," he said aloud, and his voice sounded small and hollow among the rocks. "No!" he shouted with all the force he could muster.

There must be a way out ... a way to get back to Evelyn. I can't give in, for both our sakes.

He tried to think. Checked each of his limbs in turn, testing the give of the rocks that encased him. He tried to detach himself from his fear, to think of himself as his father's creation, limbs and organs rebuilt and improved. There was pain everywhere, but he didn't think any bones were broken. And pain was nothing but electrical signals. This was just a puzzle, a problem to be solved. "Test and adapt," Victor Frankenstein would have said. He shifted a little on to his side, pressure digging into his hip. Found more room, and managed to lift his knee a fraction. He heard a tiny scattering of loose rock and felt a surge of triumph.

Then a new thought occurred. If the rockfall was unstable, one wrong move might bring more down on him and finish him off. Crush his skull, or pierce his internal organs. It might not be a quick death.

Talk about being stuck between a rock and a hard place.

On the other hand, Evelyn and the others might not have quick deaths either, if Draka reached them.

He strove frantically for a few seconds, working his leg up and down. So what if a rock killed him? Better to die by his own mistake, at least trying to escape, rather than waiting for Draka to come back and take his soul.

He kicked with all the strength he could muster, and his foot broke through into empty space. *That's it. Now for an arm.* The lightning blade was over a thousand degrees at its core, enough to melt sandstone. He could use it to cut through the rock. But it was still stuck. He focused his mind away from all other thoughts and willed it to extend. Then he wriggled his hand from side to side, twisting the metal of the housing to give the blade more leeway. Chips of rock trickled among the larger stones. Luke clenched his jaw and strained, feeling the metal twist. At last the lightning blade shot out, and the whole pile of rubble shifted. Luke blinked as dust showered into his face. He took a huge breath of cool air.

Just one big heave and he'd be free, he was sure. But he

had no idea if his enhanced strength would be enough. He knew he could bench-press a tonne with ease, but this was entirely different. Fear and pain sapped his strength. He waited a few seconds, taking bigger and bigger lungfuls of air. Steadying his mind.

Now!

He tensed his whole body and drove his arms upward. The rocks across his chest and shoulders burst outwards, and with a roar Luke clambered out, gasping as he rolled on to all fours.

The chamber was unrecognisable. The door just a jagged hole a few feet across. The white chests were buried out of sight. Luke had cuts and abrasions across his body, and his clothes were torn. But he was alive.

And there was his satchel, sticking out from a pile of small rocks. With a pang of dread, Luke pulled it out and looked inside.

His heart leapt as he saw that the equipment was undamaged.

"This isn't over yet," he muttered.

Without any more delay, he scrambled through the remains of the door.

Many of the pendula were on the ground, broken, as if Draka had simply thrust them aside. The force field fizzed and sparked, a hole smashed through its centre.

He's more powerful than we could ever have imagined,

thought Luke. Despite all the aches and pains, he sprinted to the edge and jumped the gap with ease. He sprinted as fast as he could back through the cave passageway. Through his ocular lens he made out the hot patches of Draka's footsteps, gradually fading from the rocky floor. He kicked harder. At last, light began to flood the passage, and then he burst out of the cave entrance into . . .

Everything had changed in the moonlit clearing. The ground was barren and covered in pale dust. The trees were black and wilted, their branches dead and drooping. The bodies of dead alligators lay about on their backs, decomposing already. It was as if a wave of death had passed through.

And there was no sign of Evelyn. Or Raziel and Dodger.

He could hear the sound of a desperate cry – a wail growing in volume by the second. Then a black shape landed with a thump in the clearing, sliding across the ground and fetching up against the base of a dead mangrove. It was Dodger.

With a moan of pain, he sat up, replaced his crumpled hat, and looked at Luke blearily.

"Oh, you're alive," he said. "We could do with a hand."

"Where's Evel—" Luke began.

Trees straight ahead began to snap and collapse as Draka crashed through. He was locked in combat with Raziel, towering over the gargoyle as they bulldozed through the trunks. The gargoyle had both hands around Draka's throat, but Draka was clawing at his face and driving the gargoyle back.

The two grappling giants rolled into the clearing, and Draka managed to get on top. He smashed Raziel's hands aside. Two more elbows to Raziel's face left the gargoyle dazed and reeling. Luke swung off his satchel and searched inside. Draka reached over his back and plucked an arrow from his quiver, then raised the arm to stab with the point. Luke's fingers clasped round the grenade. He pulled it out, flicked off the pin, then hurled it at Draka's head . . .

A huge red hand jerked up and caught it, leaving Luke open-mouthed.

"Your puny weapons amuse me," said Draka. He closed his fist over the grenade and it exploded within. Draka looked at the mangled stump of his wrist and grinned as it began to reform. In just a few seconds, his hand was as new.

"All right, clever clogs," said Dodger. "No need to show off." He turned to Luke, muttering, "Evelyn's back by the water. We hid her in the boat." Then he charged in to attack, and even Luke's eyes couldn't follow every dart and duck and weave. By the time Dodger stopped, Draka was encircled with a wire, arms pinned to his side. Dodger was breathing hard – moving like that drained him severely, Luke knew. "Trussed up like a Christmas turkey," he panted.

Draka grunted, lifting his arms and snapping the wire

easily. Dodger rolled his eyes, then choked as Draka grabbed him by the collar and lifted him off his feet. "Finished?" said Draka.

Raziel had managed to scramble free. "Go Luke!" the gargoyle shouted, before he bowled into Draka, driving him backwards.

For a second Luke hesitated. Then he turned from the fight and ran through the trees, back the way they had come.

He found Evelyn fetched up against a bank of mud. She had her staff across her chest, but he realised she was barely able to lift it. Her face was skeletal. But at least she was still conscious.

"Sorry, Luke," she slurred. "I'm not much use."

Luke put his fingers to his lips as he crouched beside her, shrugging off his satchel. "We're going to fix you," he said. "Just stay still."

He withdrew the equipment, unhooked the various cannulas and wires, donned latex gloves, and pulled back Evelyn's sleeve.

"Don't like needles," she said, with a weak smile.

Luke worked quickly and efficiently, without speaking. He inserted the wires into arteries and veins across her body – arm, leg, neck, under her armpit. He didn't have time to re-sterilise the equipment, but if he succeeded, her natural vampirism would repel infection anyway. He had the plans memorised but checked the diagram in his scrapbook from time to time anyway. One wrong puncture, one valve left open, and the procedure would kill her. In just a couple of minutes, all the pieces were in place. He made sure the battery was charged.

"I feel like a pincushion," she said.

Luke smiled. "That's what my dad said."

A shout through the trees. *Dodger.* "Luke – he's coming for you!"

Cold terror gripped hold of Luke. He rose in front of Evelyn to see Draka crashing towards him, yellow eyes burning from behind his bull skull helmet. The Soul Hunter blasted trees aside with blue bolts of energy. Dodger and Raziel were nowhere to be seen. *It's just me now.*

The Soul Hunter seemed to have grown larger still, towering a good three metres tall.

Luke stood his ground, protecting his friend. Behind his back he clutched the sharpened end of the cannula. *If I can get him close, stab this into his arm and hit the switch . . .*

Draka paused a few giant strides away, cocked his head and gazed at Evelyn. "So this is who you are protecting. A blood-sucker?"

"Come and get her," said Luke, taunting him.

"Her body is weak," said Draka, sniffing at the air, "but her soul is strong." His gaze rested on Luke. "Move aside, and I will grant you a quick death."

"No way," said Luke.

Draka roared and blasted Luke with a beam of blue light. Agonising heat erupted across his skin, and it felt like his insides were melting. He was only dimly aware of being lifted off the ground and hurled through the air. He landed with a thump in the shallows of the swamp. The magical energy left Luke's bones aching. He fought against the sucking mud, dragging himself back to shore. He couldn't let Evelyn die. He watched in horrible slow motion as Draka stood over his friend's body.

"I'm not scared of you!" she croaked.

Luke tried to clamber to his feet, but slipped over.

Draka drew an arrow. "Then you are a fool."

Too far away, Luke staggered helplessly.

There was nothing he could do.

CHAPTER 18

A dark shape pounced from the trees, crashing into Draka's shoulder and knocking him to the ground. Right where Evelyn lay.

No!

Praying the equipment wasn't damaged, Luke found an extra ounce of strength and launched himself clear of the water. Draka was wrestling with his attacker in the mud, a ball of red flesh and snarling fur. They fell apart, and Luke saw it was a huge werewolf, its muzzle bloody. It turned its eyes on him, glinting with intelligence, and he knew the black-eyed stare at once.

"Aurora!" he said.

She stalked Draka in a circle, as the Soul Hunter's torn shoulder sealed itself. He flexed his neck.

"My old foe," he said. "How I have longed for you."

Luke ran behind her, towards Evelyn. With a rush of

relief he saw his friend was still alive, on her side. The cannulas had come loose though, and the battery was covered in mud. He skidded to a halt beside her.

"You need to wound him!" Luke said to Aurora. "Hold him down. It's the only way to save Evelyn."

Aurora tipped back her head and howled. Luke's heart lifted as he saw more werewolves approaching through the trees. At least a dozen, grey and brown and black, all sizes, all padding menacingly.

He had to get Evelyn away from danger, while the werewolves fought Draka. Luke spread his arms beneath her and lifted her into the boat. As he picked up the battery, it rattled ominously.

Draka drew an arrow, almost casually, and placed it to his bow. He drew back the bowstring.

Luke heard the twang and one werewolf flew backwards as a silver-tipped arrow punched through its chest. It whined horribly, writhing, then lay still. Luke watched, half in amazement, half in horror, as a white smoke left its body and flowed across the clearing into Draka's mouth.

He's consuming the soul.

Draka breathed in deeply.

Luke shoved the boat back on to the water, and jumped in, turning to watch as all the wolves sped forward in a pack, eating up the ground between the trees in huge bounds. Draka smoothly nocked another arrow and fired. A werewolf dropped in mid-air, dead.

With a howl, Aurora landed on the Soul Hunter's back, raking her claws down the alligator armour. Draka fell to his knees, and hope welled inside Luke that he might be weakening. Two more wolves – one red-furred and wiry, the other dark and muscular – ploughed into him. Luke saw snapping, tearing teeth. Three more joined, their backs flexing as they closed their teeth over red limbs, tugging and shaking. *If they can hold him there . . .*

Draka stood up and the creatures hung from him. One by one, he grabbed handfuls of their fur and ripped them free, leaving deep wounds in his flesh that healed instantly. Luke's hope dissolved. Draka picked up the bow he'd dropped, and brandished it like a fighting staff. He caught werewolves across the legs, tripping them, and one across the jaw. It fell on to its back, and Draka buried an arrowhead into its gut, drinking its spirit as it died.

Evelyn was a dead weight, but Luke felt a pulse at her neck. A weak one. Her head shook as if she was having a bad dream. "Don't give up," he said. "Please." But as Luke fiddled with the transfusion tubes, the truth dawned on him with a slow, sickening dread.

The transferral equipment was wrecked.

Some of the cannulas were fractured at the tips, others had torn free.

He looked up again, and saw the werewolves were down to just three – the others lay either dead, floating in the lagoon, or wounded, limping across the bank.

Draka cried out in a ravenous frenzy, bellowing through the swamps. "I will feed on your soul!" He punched an arrow right through the middle of a werewolf. He managed to get another by the head as it tore at his face. With a brutal twist, he broke its neck and devoured its soul in a rasping breath. Aurora strode up the bank of the swamp, blood trickling from wounds on her flank. She paused for a moment, as if shocked, then her muzzle snarled and she pounced in again. Draka met her with a kick that sent her sprawling. He paced after her, drawing an arrow to finish her off. Luke watched from the boat, unable to do anything. He had no grenades left.

The sky seemed to darken as the Soul Hunter prepared to devour his friend . . .

Then, with a deafening *boom*, a flash of light hit Draka in the chest, blowing him back. *Lightning*, Luke realised, shocked. Then Luke saw a woman in the sky. He zoomed in with his ocular lens and made out a stern face, crisscrossed with wrinkles so fine they could have been scored by a needle. The woman floated through the air above the trees, mouth set in a determined line.

Marie Le Roux. The witch! It must be. "Blast him!" Luke bellowed.

Draka managed to stop himself at last. "Be gone, witch!" he said, and thrust out his own arms, unleashing a blue beam of magical energy. As it hit Marie Le Roux, she cried out and dropped from the sky, crashing through the branches of a tree and collapsing to the ground. Luke's heart fell.

"You have no idea what I have become," said Draka. "Your spells are useless now." He gestured around at the carnage of dead and wounded werewolves. "It is only the beginning. My city awaits, and with it the souls of millions. I will rip their spirits from them, and each will become my slave. Even the dead will do my bidding."

Draka crouched, his muscles bunching, and, in a single enormous bound, crossed twenty metres of water to another spit of land. He jumped again, ripping through branches. Luke heard the crunch of his steps growing distant. Then he was gone, heading east.

Towards New Orleans.

To a massacre.

Luke pushed the boat back towards the shore. Marie Le Roux limped over, looking shaken but unharmed. "You must be Master Frankenstein," she said.

Luke nodded.

Marie pointed at Evelyn. "Your friend there . . ." she said. "She looks in a bad way."

The witch was right – Evelyn was completely still. "Is there anything you can do?" Luke asked the witch.

Marie shook her head and fixed Luke with a kind, sad gaze. "My magic can't fight death," she said.

Luke knew he had failed. Tears brimmed in his eyes, and he felt drained. It had all been for nothing. He looked up to where Aurora crouched over the bodies of the dead pack members, keening softly.

Dodger and Raziel came through the trees, supporting one another. "What did we miss?" said Dodger.

Aurora turned and growled, showing her fangs. Dodger swallowed when he saw the bodies. "Oh."

Luke looked back east, his heart aching, to where the sky was beginning to lighten as the Earth turned around its axis. Little did the people of New Orleans know, but with the dawn would come death.

Evelyn was slipping away, the last chance of saving her gone. Half of the werewolf pack was dead. He had failed. Failed Victor, failed Harker, failed his dearest friend.

It's over, and there's nothing the Immortals can do.

The Age of Draka had come.

CHAPTER 19

"The equipment is broken," Luke said quietly, crouching beside Evelyn. He didn't know if she could still hear, or if she'd lost her senses completely. Her face displayed no emotion.

"This ain't your fight now," said Marie Le Roux with resignation, drawing a deep breath. "The Soul Hunter's my problem."

Aurora growled, and Luke looked to Dodger and Raziel. "We can't let Marie go alone. We can't let Evelyn die for nothing."

Raziel nodded. "I stand with you, Master Frankenstein. To the death."

Dodger looked up at the stone giant, then shrugged. "Yeah – what he said."

Hands gripped Luke's head and Evelyn jerked up beside him, eyes flashing open and fangs bared in a snarl. He lifted

255

his arm to shield himself, and her teeth clamped into the metal framework of his forearm, visible beneath his broken skin. Marie's hands sparked into life and she pointed them at Evelyn ... "I'll put her out of her misery."

"Wait!" Luke cried, shielding his friend. "You can't kill her!" He shoved his other arm over Evelyn's throat and managed to push her off, pinning her down as she thrashed wildly.

It's like Harker all over again – the death throes brought on by the BDS.

It was remarkable to feel the power in his friend's limbs as she fought to free herself, but eventually she sagged back, lips closing over her fangs. Luke looked from his friend to Marie. The lightning magic was dying in her palms, but an idea had already taken hold in his mind, a fire fanned by desperate hope.

"Luke, you OK?" asked Dodger.

Luke blinked as his eyes drifted to the smashed-up apparatus for transference.

A bite. And lightning.

A conduit of blood, and electricity.

Maybe it didn't matter if the equipment was wrecked.

Maybe they didn't need it at all.

If I can get Evelyn to bite Draka, Marie can use her lightning to start the transferral ...

Luke's hopes guttered. It would never work, would it?

256

They'd have to get close to Draka again. And Evelyn was at death's door already. He doubted her teeth could even puncture the Soul Hunter's flesh.

It was a thousand to one, completely improbable.

But it was a chance.

He stood up. "We need to go after Draka. I think I know a way to stop him."

He quickly explained to the others. Marie pursed her lips and nodded. "Boy's right. It might work. We could drain the immortality from both Draka and the Blood Armour at the same time."

"I can carry you and Evelyn," said Raziel to Luke. "The witch as well."

"I can make my own way," said Marie, eyes twinkling.

She closed her hands over her chest and a fierce wind whipped through the mangroves, ripping off leaves and licking at Luke's clothes. But gradually it seemed to settle on Marie alone. Slowly, her feet left the ground, and the mini hurricane carried her over the trees.

"Follow me, friends," she said. At astonishing speed, she shot off through the sky.

Raziel gathered up Evelyn, who was limp again, and Luke scrambled back between his shoulder blades.

"What about me?" asked Dodger. "Am I supposed to hitch?"

"Stay with Aurora," Luke said. "Help her with the

wounded wolves, and regroup. The city will need all the protection it can get." Marie was already just a dot above the Lagoon.

Dodger peered at the slavering werewolf beside him, with an uncertain expression. "Oh marvellous," he said.

Raziel pushed off with heavy wingbeats.

"Hold on, Evelyn!" Luke shouted, clinging to the gargoyle's neck.

Just a little longer . . .

The trail wasn't hard to follow – wherever Draka had gone the trees and vegetation were wilted, blackened and rotting. They flew at the witch's side, shadowed by storm clouds, Luke holding Evelyn tight to Raziel's back. From time to time Luke looked across and saw the witch's mouth set in a determined line. And despite the task ahead – and the almost certain death that awaited – he found himself wondering about Marie Le Roux. Who she was, her history, her powers.

There'll be time for that later. If any of us survive.

They flew on into a red dawn sky, the top of the sun's burning arc peeking up above the horizon. The bayou gave way to patches of forest and more roads, making Draka's trail harder to follow. They pressed straight ahead towards the distant city. They knew where the Soul Hunter was going. His feeding ground. His vengeance.

They passed deserted warehouses, timber yards, industrial complexes, truck stops, a vast scrap metal dump.

And then the first of the houses, hundreds of acres of neat suburban bungalows laid out in rows. Innocent people in their beds, ignorant of the curse that would destroy everything they held dear. Marie slowed, surveying the vast sprawl. She was breathing heavily, Luke noticed – her magic was tiring her.

"There," said Raziel, swooping lower.

Luke saw that among the pristine lawns below, several had brown grass. A mailbox lay smashed in the middle of a road, and a car alarm was flashing. In a back yard, a dog barked madly and the swimming pool looked like a murky swamp.

He came this way for sure, Luke thought. His internal GPS told him this place was Village de L'Est.

They set down in front of a Vietnamese restaurant whose sign was hanging loose and throwing off sparks. Luke slid off Raziel's back. In the parking lot, an Asian man in a chef's outfit was looking at his car, the bonnet crushed. When he saw Raziel and the others he fled indoors.

"He's close," said Marie.

Luke edged to Raziel's side to look at Evelyn, flopped across the stone arms.

"She is still alive," said the gargoyle. "But I fear she will not be able to cooperate."

259

Luke touched Evelyn's limp hand and stroked it. "Evelyn, it's Luke. If you can hear me, hang on. When I give the word, you have to bite Draka. Please, Evelyn – I know you're in there, somewhere. Wait for my word, then bite him."

Luke thought an eyelid fluttered, but it might have simply been an involuntary movement. As they rounded a corner, he saw the street ahead filled with people – maybe thirty of them, all with their backs to him as if transfixed on some spectacle beyond. Some wore nightclothes, others were half dressed.

"What are they looking at?" he muttered.

Marie's eyes were narrowed, and she pulled Luke back. "I sense evil here."

As one, the people turned. Luke stopped in his tracks.

The citizens were all covered in wounds: gaping lacerations across their torsos, missing limbs, bruised flesh. Their clothes were bloody tatters, matching the red of their eyes.

"What are they?" said Luke.

Marie shook her head, her wrinkled eyes glistening with pity. "We're too late. Draka's killed already. And he's brought his victims back to life, under his control."

The realisation hit Luke like a blow. "Necromancy," he said. The Soul Hunter had inherited Sanakhte's powers over life and death. The power to create walking corpses.

"Why do they not attack?" said Raziel.

"They're waiting," said Marie softly. "For his command."

Luke felt an uncomfortable tingle at the back of his neck, and spun around. More zombies, closing from the other end of the street. They stopped twenty metres away.

Then a red shape dropped from the sky, crunching into the tarmac of the road in front of them and sending tremors through the ground.

Draka.

The lipless mouth stretched back over his teeth in a grin.

"You did not have to pursue your deaths with such zeal," he said. "I would have come for you when I was ready." He cast an arm towards the zombies. "These wretched creatures have whet my appetite though. Perhaps the man of stone will be next." His eyes fell on Raziel.

Luke sensed the zombies edging closer. If they attacked he could probably fight them, but Evelyn would not survive another brawl. *I might not get another chance.* He needed to distract Draka long enough for her to get close.

"Don't bother with the gargoyle," shouted Luke, moving in front of Raziel. "He's the weakest among us. Fight me!"

Draka laughed. "Foolish boy."

"Foolish?" said Luke. "You ran from this foolish *boy* in the cave. Fled like a coward."

The slashes of Draka's nostrils flared in his face. His body throbbed with anger, veins popping under his skin.

"Your words are lofty, but I sense your fear," he said. "I will drain you of your false courage."

"Come on then!" yelled Luke, slashing his lightning blade back and forth. "Let's see what you've got."

"As you wish."

"Luke . . ." Raziel began.

"No, stay back," said Luke, stepping towards Draka. "When it's time, you'll know."

Raziel eyed him with uncertainty. But Marie nodded. "Go ahead, chile."

Draka advanced, and caught Luke's lightning blade in his fist. Luke felt it sinking into the Soul Hunter's flesh. His heart raced as Draka gripped the top of his head with his free hand and lifted him off the ground. Luke felt his skull squeezed in the demon's grip, and knew the Soul Hunter could crush his brain into pulp.

"You see?" said Draka, pulling him close. The yellow, slitted eyes observed him with cold curiosity. "This is how it feels to die."

Luke reached into his pocket, fumbling in agony. His fingers closed on the grenade, and he flicked the catch.

"I've . . . been . . . dead before," he said. And he thrust the grenade down Draka's throat.

The Soul Hunter choked and the hand on Luke's skull loosened, dumping him on to the road.

"Fire in the hole!" Luke cried, then he shut his eyes, bracing himself.

A boom shook the air and scraps of something moist spattered over his clothes.

For a moment, Luke couldn't hear anything but a ringing in his ears. He opened his eyes and saw Draka on his knees, smoke drifting from the remains of his head. The red neck was a mangled, gory stump. But the Soul Hunter wasn't dead. His hands reached for the wound, flexing to feel the damage.

Raziel hurried forward, holding Evelyn carefully in his arms. Lightning sparked in Marie's hands as she lifted them.

"Now!" Luke urged. "Bite him!"

Evelyn stayed motionless, limp in the grasp of the gargoyle. The mess of Draka's head began to knit together, flesh forming into a misshapen stub.

"Do it!" Luke cried. "Please!"

Nothing.

The slash of Draka's mouth reformed, then the pits of his eyes. He was already laughing, a guttural wet sound. "You cannot kill me!" he bellowed.

With a swinging hand, he swatted Raziel aside. The gargoyle dropped Evelyn in a heap as he staggered backwards, slumping down against a garage door. Draka thrust out a hand and blasted Marie Le Roux across the road with a flash of blue light. Then he crouched down low and stabbed his claws deep into Evelyn's stomach. Luke screamed from the depths of his being.

Evelyn spasmed. Her mouth stretched wide. Then her eyes snapped open, and she sank her fangs into Draka's leg.

Luke felt a sudden searing heat as lightning slammed into the Soul Hunter's chest. He saw Marie sitting up in the road, arms shaking, focusing all her power at Draka.

Evelyn's throat bobbed as she drank deep, and Luke's hope flickered back into life. *It's working. She's draining him.*

Draka seemed pinned, arms stretched out cruciform as the light flowed into his chest. He shrieked in pain and panic, head thrashing side to side.

Then the light died, leaving echoes of rippling colour behind Luke's eyes. Evelyn fell back.

The zombies in the street dropped to the ground in perfect synchrony as Draka blinked, wobbling slightly. His body looked weaker, somehow more earthly than before. "What have you done to me?" he said.

My turn, thought Luke.

He rolled forwards and jammed his lightning blade straight through Draka's eye socket.

The sword burst through the back of the Soul Hunter's head. A red, swirling cloud flooded out of the wound. *It's*

Draka. The spirit writhed in the air, splitting apart, leaking streaks of red, which dissolved in the air. Then, with a flash, the centre of the red cloud exploded in a burst of red sparks. Nothing remained.

Draka was destroyed.

"Welcome to mortality," said Luke.

The Blood Armour stiffened, hands shuddering for a moment. Then it fell back, landing with a thud on the tarmac.

He scrambled to where Evelyn lay, her lips smeared with Draka's blood.

"Evelyn?" he said. "Evelyn?"

Her face was still pale.

She can't die, not after all this.

Then Luke saw colour creeping up her cheeks like a tide of warmth. "She's alive!" he cried. Tears sprang to his eyes.

Evelyn opened her own eyes, looked at him blearily. "Thanks to you," she said.

Luke grinned then hugged her fiercely, ignoring the aches all over his body. He quickly pulled away, realising she would be hurting worse than him. "Sorry."

Evelyn grabbed his shoulder and pulled herself to her feet. "I feel fine, actually." She dusted down her jacket. "Nothing like the power of an ancient demon to rejuvenate you." Luke eyed her curiously. He wondered exactly how the transfer had affected her abilities.

"Don't give me the Victor Frankenstein look," said Evelyn. Luke laughed. There was no doubt that she was the old Evelyn.

Raziel had clambered to his feet and approached, bowing. "Mistress Evelyn. It is good to have you back."

Evelyn patted his rocky flank. "It's good to be back, Raziel – and thanks for saving me, as well."

Marie was stood over the bodies of the dead, eyes closed, palms raised, muttering what Luke guessed was some kind of prayer under her breath.

Luke walked over. "Their souls are free at least," said the witch. She sighed, and her face was etched with sadness. Luke thought it looked even more ancient.

"You couldn't have done anything for them," he said. "And you saved the city from the reign of Draka."

"Maybe you're right, chile. His evil is gone from this world for ever." She eyed the Blood Armour coldly. "And his vessel is destroyed too."

Luke saw that the wound burned through Draka's eye socket by his lightning blade was still there. Evelyn rocked the red corpse with her boot. "Yeah. He's not coming back this time round."

Sirens blared through the streets. They weren't far off. "We should take Draka's body away," said Luke.

Marie nodded. "To the swamps. We'll let the gators see to him."

Raziel crouched and hauled up the body, shrunk in size now its spirit was destroyed. With a heave he draped it over his broad stone shoulder.

Luke located the Blind Lagoon on his in-built GPS and pointed towards the side of the road. "We can take cover if we go this way." Cotton fields stretched ahead, but he could see a dark line where the mangroves began in the distance. "Better hurry. Dodger and Aurora will be wondering if we made it."

Evelyn jumped over the ditch bordering the road and landed in the field. She glanced back at Luke. "Yeah. If they've survived each other's company."

Luke grinned. "Let's just hope he hasn't called her 'whiskers' again."

CHAPTER 20

The people sitting outside cafés and walking along the pavements all looked up as the motorcycle cortege rumbled past, two by two. Luke, sitting behind Aurora, watched the lights of the city sparkle. Music spilled from the bars, and the smells of barbecued food made his stomach rumble. Even at night, New Orleans throbbed with life.

And to think, all this could have been destroyed, consumed by the Soul Hunter. They'd come so close to failure.

But Draka was definitely dead this time. And the red flesh of his Blood Armour would be half-digested by alligators by now.

Evelyn sat on the back of another werewolf's bike – Aurora's friend called Cole – riding slowly at their side. Her eyes reflected the neon signs of the clubs and restaurants. She didn't even have any scars from the fight – so far it looked like the transfer had been a complete success. Luke's own body ached from battle, and his right arm would remain in a sling until he could get back to England and heal it properly. He was already wondering if he could improve the lightning blade when they returned to the tech labs.

Harker will know how to . . .

No. He wasn't thinking properly. Harker couldn't help with anything now.

He glanced at Evelyn again, and wondered if she was thinking something similar. Her features were serene now, but he was sure he'd heard her crying earlier, through the paper-thin wall that separated their motel rooms. Life would take a lot of adjustment.

They'd buried the bodies of the dead werewolves in the garden of an abandoned, tumbledown house on the outskirts of the city. Luke had no idea why Aurora chose that place, but she was the Alpha now. She had given a short speech about the dead, but mostly her mind seemed elsewhere. She'd kept looking up at the house, but hadn't gone inside.

The first pair of motorcycles peeled off, pulling up outside a club decorated with the flashing sign of a trumpet. Lively jazz music came through the open shutters.

"Don't much like jazz," complained Dodger, as he climbed off the back of his ride. "No tune, is there? Gimme a music hall melody over this any day of the week."

"Have some respect!" hissed Evelyn.

But Aurora gave a small smile. "Just give it a try," she said, heading up the steps. "It grows on you."

The rest of the pack trooped through the door after her. Luke wondered what Aurora would do when it came time to leave. Her pack was here in her native country. She'd avenged her brother. What could England possibly hold for her now?

Luke glanced up, by instinct, and spotted a silhouette high above, whipping through the clouds. Raziel's wing was almost healed too.

"You coming in?" said Evelyn, holding open the door.

Luke nodded. "Let's go."

The bar was rammed. The werewolves blended in well among the other clientele, a mixture of people, all ages and backgrounds. There was some festival on and many were wearing masks and costumes – birds' heads, skulls, a dragon.

"We kind of fit in here," said Luke above the music.

Evelyn laughed as a waitress in a skeleton outfit came past balancing a tray.

They followed Aurora through a thick curtain into a back room. The sounds of the band were muted here, and there was a small private bar. Cole began to pour drinks into shot glasses and the wolf pack each took one.

"Don't mind if I do," said Dodger, grabbing a glass too.

Luke noticed Marie Le Roux was sitting in a corner, watching with a contented smile.

Cole muttered something to Aurora, and she shook her head. He cleared his throat and raised his glass towards Luke and Evelyn.

"I'm not a guy with much to say, but I just want to say a thank you, to Aurora's friends. People like us, we kinda act suspicious, stick with our own kind. But Luke, Evelyn, Dodger, if you hadn't showed up, we'd all be dead." He paused. Shrugged. "That's about it."

The other werewolves lifted their glasses with a roar, then drank. Dodger sipped too, and made a disgusted face. Evelyn smirked.

The wake got raucous after that. Werewolves seemed to like two things in particular – drinking, and arm-wrestling. But Luke noticed Aurora didn't partake in either. He spent some time chatting with Evelyn – she was putting a brave face on things, talking about taking out a death notice in the *Vampire's Gazette*, and the complications of organising a proper funeral for her dad. Meanwhile Dodger showed off his best sleight-of-hand magic tricks.

When Evelyn asked to be alone for a while, Luke went to chat with Marie Le Roux. He realised he'd never met a proper witch before, and he had made a long list of questions in his notebook, hoping he might bag a few minutes to quiz her.

He found out pretty quickly that she didn't do straight

answers. Every question he asked received only a knowing smile and a cryptic response. He wrote them all down as best he could.

How did she get her powers?

"My powers got me, boy, not the other way around."

Did she have a spell book?

"If you have to write a spell down, you ain't no witch."

How long would she live?

"As long as the power of the land runs through me."

How old was she?

"You know, boy, you're kinda nosey," she said at last. "Some mysteries are better left that way."

"No they're not!" Luke protested. "That's just a saying."

"Well, I got a saying for ya," said Marie, checking her watch. "Don't stay up past midnight when you got an early shift the next day."

Luke sighed, watching the little old woman hobble out of the door. As she did, he saw Aurora on the veranda outside, standing alone. He stood and pushed through the pack of werewolves. Dodger had taken up his place at the beer-soaked arm-wrestling table, squaring up against Cole. "Don't go easy on me," he said.

"I won't," Cole replied.

Luke pushed through the door, into the warm night. Aurora was leaning over a balcony looking at the moon – now waning a fraction. Aurora must have smelled him, because she spoke his name without turning.

"Luke." She fished in her pocket and drew out a coin. A silver dime. "Got this in an antique stall today. Same year, exactly." She tossed it up and caught it flat, closing her fingers over it to hide the face. "Stay or go?" she said.

"I'm sorry?" said Luke. Evelyn emerged behind him, and Luke saw she was looking a little brighter.

"Dodger's just broken his hand," she said. "What's up?"

Luke nodded at Aurora's closed fist.

"Shall I stay here?" said Aurora. "Or come back to England?"

Luke didn't know what to say. He wanted her to come with them, to keep the team intact, but he didn't know how to ask that. He wanted to tell her that they could never replace the family she'd lost, but that they'd all lost someone dear to them, and together they were stronger. They'd proved that no one could stop them, when they acted as one.

Aurora opened up her fingers and smiled.

"What time do we fly?"

Two days later, Luke sat at his father's old desk in the study at the Stein Foundation, scribbling the last details down in his notebook. He wanted to get the whole adventure from Louisiana down while it was still fresh, and he was near the end.

The farewell to the wolf pack had been very low-key. Cole

had agreed to take over as Alpha, and sealed it with just a shake of the hand. His first job was to go to Fontaine's American lab and burn it to the ground. "No evidence," Aurora had said.

She'd slept the entire flight back, long legs crammed in economy, while Dodger had nursed his broken hand and mumbled several times that he'd just let the werewolf win, but if he ever had another chance, he'd show him who was boss.

There was a knock at the door of the study.

"Come in," said Luke.

He expected Evelyn – she'd been busy trying to arrange a wake at Clarence's, the vampire club in London. Apparently they weren't keen on non-vampire guests. But it was Dr Pavlovic who entered meekly. "Hello, Luke," she said.

"Oh, hi," he replied. He'd barely seen her since he returned, but he knew that Raziel had filled her in on all that had happened across the sea.

"Do you have a moment?" she said.

Luke put down his pen.

Dr Pavlovic blushed. "I came to ... to tender my resignation."

Luke shook his head. "You can't ... "

"I brought Dr Fontaine here. I put the entire Foundation at risk. Not to mention the entire world. It will be difficult, but I am happy to step aside and let you take over, Luke."

"No," said Luke firmly. "We all misjudged Fontaine. It wasn't your fault."

The doctor bowed her head. "But I misjudged you, too, and your friends. I was rude and defensive."

"You were confused," said Luke. "To be honest, I didn't like you either."

She looked up, smiling. "I was mistrustful. I call myself a scientist, but science is about dealing with the unexpected."

Luke smiled now. "My dad used to say the same thing. Look, you have to stay. I can see the great work the Foundation does. My dad would be proud of what it has become."

Dr Pavlovic's eyes glistened. "Thank you for saying that, but ... "

"Besides," continued Luke. "I'm an Immortal, not a CEO! We need you here."

Dr Pavlovic opened her mouth, then shut it again. After a moment, she nodded. She gestured to the shelves, still loaded with old books. "In that case, I think we should catalogue this library. Study it. There might be some things here that could offer new discoveries, new avenues of exploration." She paused. "With your permission, of course."

Luke blinked. "Great idea."

"And it would be wonderful if you could stay too," said the doctor. "You obviously have the makings of a great scientist, just like your father. He'd be proud of you."

It was Luke's turn to go bright red. "Thank you," he said, "but I can't. My place is back in London. We have to rebuild the base in the crypt. There'll be other battles."

Dr Pavlovic nodded. "I understand. But you should know – this place will always have its doors open to you. We'll have to appoint someone else to head up the Immortals research division, of course." She grimaced. "Someone more reliable this time."

"Couldn't you do it?" asked Luke.

"Me?" said Dr Pavlovic. "I'm flattered, but you need a weapons specialist."

"You're pretty handy with a grenade," said Luke, laughing.

Dr Pavlovic puffed out her cheeks. "Let me think about it," she said. "I suppose the fewer people that know about it the better, huh?"

Footsteps in the corridor.

"Still scribbling?" said Dodger, sticking his head through the door. Aurora was with him. "It was hard enough the first time. Dunno why you want to relive it all."

"Time to leave," said Aurora. "Chopper's waiting."

Luke stuffed his notebook in his battered satchel. "Goodbye, Doctor," he said to Pavlovic. "We'll be in touch."

"Goodbye, Luke," she said, and shook his hand.

Outside, Raziel stood sentinel beside the helipad. Luke ducked under the spinning rotors. He hesitated for a moment when he saw the coffin in the back. Harker's.

Evelyn was sitting in the co-pilot's seat. "Wake's booked,"

she said. "You'd be amazed by the politics involved in a vampire funeral. The feuds ..."

She grinned, but Luke could see the grief in her eyes. He knew she was just being brave. He climbed in beside her, putting on the earphones. Dodger and Aurora squeezed together in the rear.

"They've upgraded the stealth settings," said Evelyn. "Reflective hull makes us pretty much invisible."

"Great," said Luke. "I'm not sure I could stomach another chase."

Dodger groaned. "Just take it easy, will you? I had kippers for breakfast."

Evelyn snorted, and Luke laughed. For a brief moment the sombre mood was broken.

Aurora glanced at him nervously. "I second that. No stunts, please."

Luke nodded. "OK, don't worry. I'll make sure you get a smooth ride." He began to flick switches.

Soon they were soaring over the English countryside. Luke drew in a long breath, as he tweaked the steering lever. In his heart, he knew that nothing would be the same again. Jonathan Harker, leader of the Immortals, was gone. He peered at Evelyn to his side. But he knew while they stuck to the vows of the Immortals, Jonathan Harker and Victor Frankenstein's legacy would never die.

"Next stop – London."

ABOUT THE AUTHOR

Alex Marlowe lives in London in a crumbling Victorian house he thinks is haunted ... or he hopes it is. When he's not strolling the city's streets, he reads Gothic novels and has a passion for old martial arts films.